A SACRIFICE FOR LOVE

Henriet was wiping away her tears.

"What am I to do – Caterina?" she asked again in a broken little voice. "I never thought – anything like this would ever happen to me."

"I did not expect it to happen either," Caterina said. "All I can suggest is that you meet the Duke and perhaps you will find him not as horrible as you think he will be."

"If he was the Archangel Gabriel," Henriet replied, "he would still not be Fritz and Fritz is the only man who has ever mattered or will ever mean anything in my life."

She spoke sincerely and Caterina knew it was true.

At the same time she was thinking wildly how she could possibly help her friend.

How she could prevent her, as she feared she might do, from trying to commit suicide rather than marry the Duke. She was quite certain, because she knew Henriet so well, that it was something she really might do.

Other people would talk about dying, but had no intention of killing themselves.

But Henriet was impulsive and she had given her heart and, as she said, her soul to Fritz Hofer.

THE BARBARA CARTLAND
PINK COLLECTION

Titles in this series

A SACRIFICE FOR LOVE

BARBARA CARTLAND

Barbaracartland.com Ltd

ISBN 978-1-78213-334-6

Printed and bound in Great Britain
by Mimeo of Huntingdon, Cambridgeshire.

THE BARBARA CARTLAND PINK COLLECTION

Dame Barbara Cartland is still regarded as the most prolific bestselling author in the history of the world.

In her lifetime she was frequently in the Guinness Book of Records for writing more books than any other living author.

Her most amazing literary feat was to double her output from 10 books a year to over 20 books a year when she was 77 to meet the huge demand.

She went on writing continuously at this rate for 20 years and wrote her very last book at the age of 97, thus completing an incredible 400 books between the ages of 77 and 97.

Her publishers finally could not keep up with this phenomenal output, so at her death in 2000 she left behind an amazing 160 unpublished manuscripts, something that no other author has ever achieved.

Barbara's son, Ian McCorquodale, together with his daughter Iona, felt that it was their sacred duty to publish all these titles for Barbara's millions of admirers all over the world who so love her wonderful romances.

So in 2004 they started publishing the 160 brand new Barbara Cartlands as *The Barbara Cartland Pink Collection*, as Barbara's favourite colour was always pink – and yet more pink!

The Barbara Cartland Pink Collection is published monthly exclusively by Barbaracartland.com and the books are numbered in sequence from 1 to 160.

Enjoy receiving a brand new Barbara Cartland book each month by taking out an annual subscription to the Pink Collection, or purchase the books individually.

The Pink Collection is available from the Barbara Cartland website www.barbaracartland.com via mail order and through all good bookshops.

In addition Ian and Iona are proud to announce that The Barbara Cartland Pink Collection is now available in ebook format as from Valentine's Day 2011.

For more information, please contact us at:

Barbaracartland.com Ltd.
Camfield Place
Hatfield
Hertfordshire AL9 6JE
United Kingdom

Telephone: +44 (0)1707 642629
Fax: +44 (0)1707 663041
Email: info@barbaracartland.com

THE LATE DAME BARBARA CARTLAND

Barbara Cartland who sadly died in May 2000 at the age of nearly 99 was the world's most famous romantic novelist who wrote 723 books in her lifetime with worldwide sales of over 1 billion copies and her books were translated into 36 different languages.

As well as romantic novels, she wrote historical biographies, 6 autobiographies, theatrical plays, books of advice on life, love, vitamins and cookery. She also found time to be a political speaker and television and radio personality.

She wrote her first book at the age of 21 and this was called *Jigsaw*. It became an immediate bestseller and sold 100,000 copies in hardback and was translated into 6 different languages. She wrote continuously throughout her life, writing bestsellers for an astonishing 76 years. Her books have always been immensely popular in the United States, where in 1976 her current books were at numbers 1 & 2 in the B. Dalton bestsellers list, a feat never achieved before or since by any author.

Barbara Cartland became a legend in her own lifetime and will be best remembered for her wonderful romantic novels, so loved by her millions of readers throughout the world.

Her books will always be treasured for their moral message, her pure and innocent heroines, her good looking and dashing heroes and above all her belief that the power of love is more important than anything else in everyone's life.

"I have always believed in true love and dreamt about the tall handsome man who will sweep me off my feet and we will live happily ever after, but I can assure that when true love finally comes to you it is always far better than the dreams."

Barbara Cartland

CHAPTER ONE
1879

Princess Caterina took the note that the servant was presenting to her on a silver salver and opened it quickly.

There was very little for her to read, just the words,

"*I must see you. Please, dearest Caterina, come to me at once.*

Henriet."

She read it through twice before she said to the servant,

"Tell the groom who brought this letter that I will come to the Palace of Istria as soon as possible."

The servant bowed and hurried from the room and Caterina wondered what could possibly be the trouble.

Was there perhaps some crisis?

Princess Henriet of Istria was her great friend.

But as they lived in separate, though neighbouring Provinces, Caterina usually only ever went to the Palace of Istria when she was invited.

Princess Henriet had not sent for her for some time and, as she knew that she would have to stay the night, she hurried upstairs and instructed her lady's maid to pack her a suitcase.

"Will Your Highness be staying for long then?" the lady's maid asked.

Caterina shook her head.

"I don't think so, but put in an extra dress or two in case I do."

Then she walked downstairs to write a note to her father to tell him that she was going to Istria.

Prince Otto was not of great political significance and he was seldom asked to the Palace and was therefore delighted when his daughter received an invitation.

"*I don't know why Henriet requires me,*" Caterina wrote to him, "*but you will understand, Papa, I must stay for as long as she wants me.*"

With the note finished, she ordered a chaise to take her to the Palace.

Then she changed out of her dress into something smarter and which had a really attractive hat to go with it.

Princess Caterina was exceedingly pretty.

In fact, she resembled her mother, who was now dead and was hailed as one of the most beautiful women in Austria. It had been a great surprise to everyone when she married Prince Otto, who was not considered nearly senior enough for her.

However, the Emperor of Austria had given them his blessing without making any difficulties.

Theirs was a small Principality with a large and impressive Palace and Prince Otto and his wife were happy in it, making the garden a picture of flowers.

They also rode on the best horses the Prince could afford over what was now his domain on succeeding his father to the throne.

When Caterina was born, they were thrilled and delighted to have her, although the Prince had, of course, hoped for a son.

Unfortunately there seemed to be no chance of any other children and so they gave Caterina all the love and attention that she might have had to share with brothers and sisters.

She had grown up, becoming more beautiful year by year and her mother was soon discussing with her father where they would find a charming but influential husband for their precious daughter.

"There is plenty of time for that," the Prince said, "and you know, darling, whoever I may suggest, you will demand someone better!"

His wife had laughed and kissed him and for the moment they forgot Caterina's future and thought only of themselves.

She was perfectly happy with her father's horses and the dogs which were allowed in the house.

Other people kept dogs in kennels, but her parents wanted their dogs with them and they were as much a part of the family as their delightful daughter.

When her mother died unexpectedly one really cold winter, Caterina realised that her father was broken-hearted and tried in every way to fill her mother's place.

Aged eighteen she was running the Palace for him and she chose the special dishes he enjoyed with the chef.

She rode with him and learnt to fish and shoot, so that she could accompany him when he was alone.

Fortunately, as he was very popular and extremely charming, Prince Otto had a great number of friends and they too tried to make things easier for him after he became a widower.

Caterina arranged all his dinner parties and, as her father loved her so much, she was hostess even when he entertained only his men friends.

It was a strange life for a young girl, but, as she was very intelligent, it made her understand others older than herself, besides enabling her to keep up with conversation, because she read so many books and newspapers.

It was not surprising that Henriet, the Princess of Istria, should turn to her when she was in trouble.

A great number of people asked Caterina for her advice and Henriet seldom took a serious step without her guidance.

It was because Caterina was so keen on learning so many subjects that Henriet had agreed that she must learn them too and her father had engaged the very best Tutors.

They had both learnt French from a teacher who taught them to speak in Parisian French and he instructed them so perfectly that when they visited France no one guessed for a moment that was not their mother tongue.

They also had a German Tutor and then finally an English one and, when he left, he boasted that they were both perfectly fluent.

"No one in England, if you ever go there," he told them, "will think that you are foreigners."

But Caterina had not seen so much of Henriet lately as she had when they were both younger.

This had not particularly disturbed her, except that she was very fond of her friend and rather missed spending much of her time in the Palace at Istria.

"I expect," her father said, "Henriet now has so many suitors that she has little time for her girlfriends."

Caterina had laughed.

"I was thinking the same, Papa, and, of course, as she is very pretty besides being of such social significance, I should imagine that all the unmarried heirs to a throne are considering what benefits they would obtain from having an Austrian bride."

Prince Otto had looked serious for a short moment before saying,

"I think the answer to that is that they are afraid of having too many."

"Too many, Papa?" Caterina enquired.

"Austria has been becoming so strong lately that a great number of European countries are afraid of her and I think the Emperor has frightened quite a number of them."

Caterina was aware of the political situation, so she had merely remarked,

"Then I hope that Henriet finds someone she really loves."

"I hope so too, but you know as well as I do, my dearest, that, when Royalty marry, they must think of duty to their country rather than the person they are marrying."

Caterina knew this to be true and she hoped to see Henriet soon and hear if any were approaching her.

She drove away in a comfortable carriage drawn by four perfectly matched horses.

She thought that perhaps Henriet had been asked to marry the heir to some throne and if so, she hoped that it would be a country whose language they had so diligently and painstakingly learnt.

She drove through the beautiful countryside with the sun shining on the lakes and trees and as she did so she was trying to think of which country would wish to be affiliated with Austria.

Henriet's father was a nephew of the Emperor of Austia and this meant it was a matter of great importance when it came to the marriage of his daughter.

Unfortunately there were, at the moment, very few Crown Princes who would be acceptable to the Emperor and Caterina found it difficult to think of any Prince of the right age whom the Emperor would approve of.

There was no one in Holland and the Russians had a great number of Princes, but none of them was a direct heir to the Czar.

The same applied in Germany where the children of the reigning Monarch were hardly out of the nursery.

'It's not going to be easy,' she thought to herself. 'Perhaps I am just imagining that is the reason why Henriet has sent for me. In fact I may find that she merely wants me to help her choose her clothes or maybe attend a ball.'

Then she decided to wait for the information when she arrived.

The Palace was looking magnificent in the golden sunshine and the garden, although not as beautiful as her own at home, was ablaze with colour.

The carriage drew up at the front door.

To Caterina's surprise, Henriet ran down the steps to greet her.

The two girls kissed and Henriet exclaimed,

"It's angelic of you to come at once, I was so afraid that you would refuse and I want you so desperately."

"Of course I will always come when you want me," Caterina replied. "What has happened? What is wrong?"

Henriet looked over her shoulder and replied,

"Don't say a word until we are alone. I told Papa I wanted to give a party and have asked you to come to help me to choose the guests."

Feeling a little bewildered, Caterina said nothing more until they were in Henriet's private rooms.

They were at the far end on the first floor and it was a very comfortable suite with large bow windows looking out over the garden on one side and the lake on the other.

The sun was streaming in through the windows and because Caterina knew it so well she felt almost as if she had come home.

Henriet had followed her into the room and was now closing the door.

Then, as she walked towards her, Caterina asked,

"What has upset you? I can see you are worried."

"I am very worried and I thought, dearest, that you would be the only one who would be able to help me."

"Of course I will help you if I can. But what has happened?"

Henriet paused for a second and then said almost in a whisper,

"I am in love."

Caterina gave a little cry.

"Oh, Henriet, how exciting, it is just what I hoped would happen to you. Who is it?"

"That is the whole point," Henriet replied.

"Why? What's wrong?"

"Nothing is wrong except that he is not important and I know that Papa will never let me marry him."

"Who is he?" Caterina enquired breathlessly.

Henriet again looked over her shoulder at the door and then whispered,

"Fritz Hofer. He is a Major in Papa's own Regiment."

Caterina knew who he was. In fact he was a very handsome and impressive-looking man and she was not in the least surprised that Henriet, who had obviously seen him often, was in love.

But she knew only too well that Henriet's father, Prince Adolphus, would not allow his daughter to marry an ordinary soldier.

"I am sorry, dearest," she said, "I can see it is going to be difficult."

"It is worse than that – "

"In what way?" Caterina asked.

"There is someone else Papa wants me to marry."

Caterina's eyes opened even wider, but she waited without asking the obvious question.

"He is an Englishman, a Duke."

"*A Duke!*" Caterina exclaimed, "but surely your father will want you to marry Royalty."

"Well the Duke is Royal in that his mother was Princess Lillian of Saxe-Coburg and a very close friend of Queen Victoria."

Caterina remembered that Queen Victoria had been married to Prince Albert of Saxe-Coburg and the Duke was therefore related to the Queen.

"And the Duke wants to marry you?" she asked her, trying to clarify the whole story in her mind.

"I have not met him yet," Henriet said, "but it has all been arranged by the Emperor who is very anxious for us to have a close tie with Great Britain."

"Have you been told that you must marry him?"

"He is on his way now to stay with us and Papa told me last night that he is going to propose to me."

Henriet gave a deep sigh before she went on,

"Both the Emperor and Queen Victoria think that it would be an excellent match, forming a tie between the two countries."

"But you are in love with someone else," Caterina said softly.

"I love Fritz. I love him with all my heart," Henriet murmured. "And he loves me."

Caterina looked at her without asking her any more questions.

Then Henriet continued,

"We meet each other secretly at night in the garden and sometimes when it has been safe in parts of the Palace where no one goes after dark.

"Fritz loves me because I am me and not because I am a Princess. I love him because he is the most charming, handsome and wonderful man in the whole world!"

She clasped her hands together and looked towards Caterina as she pleaded,

"Help me, Caterina. What can I do? How can I marry anyone else when I really love Fritz?"

Because Caterina loved Henriet, she kissed her very gently and said,

"I will help you in every way I can. But for the moment I cannot think of a solution. I suppose there is no chance of your being allowed to refuse the Duke?"

"As far as I can make out, the Emperor has already told him that he is really delighted at the idea and he will do everything he can to put my country, by this marriage, under the protection of Great Britain."

"I suppose the real reason behind all this," Caterina said, "is that they are frightened of the Russians who are making so much trouble in the Balkans. Also I suppose Germany is now so strong and perhaps dangerous since the unification of all its small Kingdoms and Principalities."

Henriet, who had never been particularly interested in politics, said,

"I don't care what they do about the country. It's *me* I am worrying about."

"Of course you are, dearest, but I cannot think for the moment what you can do."

There was silence and then Caterina enquired,

"Have you told your father that you have no wish to marry anyone you have never even met and know nothing about?"

"Papa was totally elated at the suggestion of this marriage which he received from the Emperor himself. As you can imagine, he did not even ask me what I felt about it, let alone ask for my consent."

"Oh, poor Henriet. I have always understood that Emperors and Kings do behave like this, but never thought I would actually see it happening in our lives."

"Well, it's happening in mine! Oh, Caterina, you have to help me! I cannot marry this man! I would rather kill myself."

"You are not to talk like that. You know how much you mean to me and so many people love you."

"So does Fritz," Henriet cried, "and I love him too with all my heart and soul. No other man could ever mean anything to me."

Caterina sighed.

"But, my dearest, you will have to try to like your husband, whoever he is."

"If he is not Fritz, I will hate him and I will do everything to make him hate me, so that he does not want to touch me."

She then jumped up from the sofa where they were sitting and walked towards the window.

"How can I let any man touch me except Fritz? As he has said, we belong to each other so closely that we are already one person."

Caterina could not help thinking that was exactly the way people should feel when they were in love and, of course, that was exactly what every woman would wish her husband to say to her.

"What shall I do? What shall I do?" Henriet asked wildly.

"When is the Duke arriving?" Caterina asked.

"*Tonight!* He is coming here to dinner and he has already told Papa that he would like the marriage to take place as soon as possible – as he has many important duties to perform in England. The Queen finds him so useful that he has promised her that he will be away for as short a time as possible."

"So he intends to marry you at once," Caterina said, feeling it could not be true.

"From what Papa has said, I have only a few days to put my trousseau together before leaving with the Duke for to England. Oh, Caterina – what can I do? Where can I run to – where they will not find me?"

She then threw herself down beside Caterina on the sofa and burst into tears.

Caterina put her arms round her.

"It's no use crying," she said. "We have to think of some clever way to save you, but you realise what that will mean?"

"It will mean," Henriet sobbed, "that I – will surely be thrown out of the Palace – and made an exile. But – I don't care."

Her tears choked her for a moment and then she went on,

"Fritz is rich and we will not starve. We will have – to live in another country, but that does not worry him."

"But you cannot do it, you just cannot. Think of the scandal it will cause and all the trouble there will be."

11

"I will not marry this English Duke. You must tell me how I can escape with Fritz before the ring is actually – on my finger."

Caterina looked at her and held her closer.

"It's no use crying, dearest, it's no use making wild statements. We have to think of this quietly and seriously to see what we can do."

"What can we do?" Henriet sobbed. "If I tell Papa – I will not marry the Duke, he will force me to do it – somehow. I am sure – he will."

Caterina took her arms from round her friend and rose from the sofa. She walked over to the window and looked out at the garden.

The flowers were very beautiful, but she thought that however beautiful the surroundings were, it was cruel to force someone as sensitive as Henriet to marry a man she had not even seen.

Not only to Prince Adolphus but to the Emperor, it was the country that counted. Women were just pawns in their hands to be manipulated so they could win the game.

And what the poor pawn felt was of no relevance whatsoever.

Yet, because she was so well read, Caterina could understand the situation.

Balkan rulers were continually appealing to Queen Victoria to send them a bride who would enable them to fly the Union Jack and they could then defy the Russians!

Now almost the same applied to Austria.

The Russians so far had left her alone, but they were extending their Empire and they were already on the frontier of much of Austria.

Austria had gained a certain amount of territory in the past years, but at this very moment Russia undoubtedly presented a menace they could not ignore.

From what she had read, Caterina was aware that the Russians had no wish to fight Great Britain. In point of fact they could not afford to do so.

That was why each endangered Balkan Principality begged Queen Victoria to save them and this Her Majesty could do by sending them a British Queen to fly the Union Jack beside their flag. Even the Emperor of Austria had encouraged nearby small Principalities to do the same.

It was no use, Caterina thought, explaining all this to Henriet as she would not listen.

She was in love and because Caterina knew her so well, she was sure that it was no passing fancy and that everything Henriet did she did wholeheartedly and with her mind, her body and her soul.

That was very obviously how she loved Major Fritz Hofer.

"Are you really certain," she asked, "that, if you quarrel with your father over this, Major Hofer will still love you and want you?"

"Of course he will. He has already begged me to run away with him, but I am so afraid that, as he is in the Army, he will be dragged back and certainly arrested, if not shot as a deserter."

Caterina drew in her breath.

This would be a terrible thing to happen and it would destroy Henriet's happiness for the rest of her life.

There really seemed no alternative to her accepting the decision of the Emperor and her father, but she felt that the way they were handling it was positively brutal.

'The country may mean everything to them,' she mused, 'but surely they cannot expect Henriet to feel the same as they do about it?'

Henriet was wiping away her tears.

"What am I to do – Caterina?" she asked again in a broken little voice. "I never thought – anything like this would ever happen to me."

"I did not expect it to happen either," Caterina said. "All I can suggest is that you meet the Duke and perhaps you will find him not as horrible as you think he will be."

"If he was the Archangel Gabriel," Henriet replied, "he would still not be Fritz and Fritz is the only man who has ever mattered or will ever mean anything in my life."

She spoke sincerely and Caterina knew it was true.

At the same time she was thinking wildly how she could possibly help her friend.

How she could prevent her, as she feared she might do, from trying to commit suicide rather than marry the Duke. She was quite certain, because she knew Henriet so well, that it was something she really might do.

Other people would talk about dying, but had no intention of killing themselves.

But Henriet was impulsive and she had given her heart and, as she said, her soul to Fritz Hofer.

She was therefore perfectly capable of dying rather than lose him by being forced to marry the Duke.

'What can I do to help?' Caterina asked herself.

There seemed to be nothing, but nothing she could do and then, as Henriet continued to cry, she suddenly sat up,

"I think I know what we can do."

"What is that?" Henriet asked weakly.

"We must meet the Duke and see if there is any chance of his being on your side rather than your father's. We will not have to ask him questions, we will know when we meet him what kind of man he is."

"You think he might agree that we are not suited to each other and might then return to England without me?" Henriet asked hopefully.

"It's just a chance. If you like, I will talk to him and tell him that you are in love with someone else."

"Oh, Caterina, if you did that, perhaps he will agree and make his excuses to the Emperor."

Caterina thought that this was most unlikely, but it would give her time to think and plan some other way out.

Although so far it seemed impossible, there could be one and she could not leave her friend so unhappy.

Or risk her taking her life, as she might easily do.

'I can only pray,' she thought to herself, 'that I can find some way out of this. I am sure there must be one.'

She walked to the window again as if the flowers in the garden below somehow gave her strength.

But she knew that what she was up against was almost insoluble.

If the Emperor had decided to accept the Duke and so did Prince Adolphus, then no pleadings, no arguments and certainly no threats would move them.

Her father had often laughed at the pomposity of those in authority and he had at the same time admitted that they were right in doing what was best for the country, even though a great number of people thought differently.

"If you don't have strong Rulers who are firm and determined when it comes to diplomacy," he said, "you can be quite certain that their countries will either fade into insignificance or be conquered by someone tougher than they are."

Caterina would often argue with him because they both enjoyed what her father called 'a duel with words' and yet she had to admit that he nearly always won.

She knew that he, like a great number of others who were regularly at Court, was extremely worried.

The behaviour of the Germans and Russians was completely unacceptable and it spelt danger to their weaker neighbours.

On more than one occasion Prince Otto had been proved right in saying, 'only a strong arm would make the Russians behave themselves'.

He had been proved right when the Russian Army was within six miles of Constantinople and Queen Victoria had sent six Ironclads up the Dardenelles into the Sea of Marmara.

On that occasion Britain had made her stance very clear that, if the Grand Duke Nicholas went any further, he would be obliged to fight the British as well as the Turks.

The Grand Duke on being forced to turn back had said miserably,

"The British have cost me one hundred thousand trained men and more than that in money. There is one thing I am quite certain of, I am unable to fight them."

It was obvious, Caterina thought, that under the circumstances, Austria would welcome British support and if the great-niece of the Emperor was married to a relative of Queen Victoria, what could be a better way of warning the Russians to go no further?

She could see it all happening.

But the one who suffered most would be Henriet.

'I just have to do something for her,' Caterina told herself. 'I have to.'

But for the moment she could think of nothing but what she had just suggested and not very confidently.

The girls sat talking until one of the equerries came into the Princess's sitting room.

"I am sorry to disturb Your Highness," he began, "but the Duke of Dunlerton is expected to arrive in a quarter-of-an-hour. His Royal Highness asks if you will be in the hall to greet him."

Then he saw Caterina and smiled,

"I did not know Your Highness had arrived," he said, "but it's very nice to see you again."

"I am delighted to be back at the Palace," Caterina replied.

As soon as he had left the room, she said to Henriet,

"Now come along. You have to look your best and behave as if nothing has happened to upset you."

"Why should I do that?" Henriet asked.

"Because if your father should suspect that we are plotting against the Duke and trying to fight him, it will be impossible for us to do anything, although at the moment I have no idea what that can be."

Henriet was sensible enough to realise that this was true and then she replied,

"All right, I will change and wash."

"And wipe away your tears," Caterina suggested. "Be smiling and look pleased to see him."

"But I hate him! I am *not* pleased to see him!"

"I know that," Caterina answered. "But if he is at all suspicious, then everyone else there will be suspicious too and it will make it impossible for us to do or plan anything to avoid your marriage."

Henriet realised that this was common sense.

"All right, Caterina, I will do exactly as you tell me, but I warn you I will want to scream when I see him and run as fast as I can to find my beloved Fritz."

"If you do anything like that Fritz will undoubtedly be arrested and thrown into prison."

Henriet stared at her in dismay.

"If there is the slightest suspicion that you are even flirting with him, he will then be posted away somewhere miles away and perhaps you will never see him again."

She was speaking to her firmly because she knew how hysterical Henriet could be.

She was well aware that Prince Adolphus would do anything in his power to prevent there being any scandal or any opposition to the Emperor's wishes.

The two girls went into Henriet's bedroom and she washed her face without sending for her lady's maid, as they knew that servants always talked.

Then she changed into one of her prettiest gowns and Caterina made her put on some of her mother's most glamorous jewellery.

"You have to look Regal and just remember that he represents Britain, a country which is now very important to this part of the world."

"So you have always said, but I have not listened," Henriet moaned.

"Well, you will have to listen now," Caterina said, "and act your part until we can find some way out for you. I think if we pray hard enough we will succeed."

"I will pray, of course I will pray," Henriet replied. "I pray endlessly that Fritz will love me and he does."

"Then you must pray that by some miracle you can be with him, but it is not going to be easy, dearest, to work a miracle. So the only course we can take at the moment is to pray for one."

"I will do that, I will pray all night that somehow I can escape the Duke and marry Fritz," Henriet asserted.

She spoke determinedly.

Then Caterina put her fingers to her lips.

"Be careful," she cautioned. "If people hear you say that, you know as well as I do, it would be repeated all over the Palace."

Henriet gave a cry of horror as Caterina went on,

"What you have to do is force yourself to smile and look pleased to see him. Then he will enjoy being here."

"If I could put poison in his food, I would do so!" Henriet declared.

"You must not even think of such things in case he can read your thoughts," Caterina said. "Just think about Fritz and remember that he is a soldier in your father's Army and therefore particularly vulnerable."

There was silence and then Henriet said slowly,

"You know I would do nothing to hurt him."

"As I have just warned you, if your father guesses that he has any affection for you or you for him, he will be posted away immediately."

Henriet gave a cry of sheer horror, but Caterina continued,

"Whatever you do, you must be careful for the sake of the man you love. You must not for one moment let anyone except me know what you are feeling."

"Fritz has always been careful to avoid arousing any gossip in the Palace. That was, of course, before I was told about the Duke."

"Have you told Fritz?" Caterina asked.

"I sent him a note at the same time as I sent you one," Henriet replied. "But he has not been able to answer me, except by sending a large bouquet of flowers, which I know came from him, although there was no name with it."

"Then he is being very sensible," Caterina replied approvingly, "and you have to be sensible too. What I will do, if it is possible, is to have a private conversation with

Major Hofer myself. I can perhaps tell one of the equerries that I have a message for him from my father. There is no reason why Papa should not know him."

"That is a good idea," Henriet said. "I think he did say once that he had met your father. It was at a shooting party or perhaps a race meeting."

"Then that makes it easy. You must just leave it for the moment in my hands and promise me that you will be as charming and nice to the Duke as if Fritz did not exist."

There was a short pause before Henriet replied,

"I will try, I really will try. And, dearest Caterina, you must think of some magical way I can escape."

"First things first. Now we must go downstairs and wait to meet the Duke. Let me look at you."

She stood in front of her friend and looked carefully at her face.

"I would know that you have been crying," she said, "but I don't think anyone else will. And if you smile you look very very pretty and that is what the Duke must see when he arrives."

"It's going to be difficult when I want to spit at him and tell him to go back to where he comes from."

"Hush! Be careful!" Caterina admonished. "Don't say such things even to me. It would be disastrous if the Duke or anyone else could read your thoughts."

"You are not suggesting he is as clever as you are?"

"I have no idea. He may be a stupid Englishman, which I believe some of them are or he may be extremely clever and a diplomat and anxious that neither the Russians nor the Germans will gain the upper hand."

She saw by the expression in Henriet's eyes that she was not concerned with the ambitions of either of these countries, only her own fate.

"Now come along," Caterina urged. "You know you can act as well as anyone on the stage when you want to. Remember the plays we used to perform as children to amuse your father and how much he enjoyed them. If you could act then, you can act now when your whole future happiness is at stake."

"I do know what you are saying to me," Henriet sniffed, "and I promise I will do my best."

Caterina kissed her.

"No one could ask for more," she said.

They opened the door and started to walk down the stairs.

Even as they did so they saw below them in the hall a number of Officials hurrying towards the front door.

And this could only mean that the Duke's carriage, which had carried him from the ship, had arrived.

As they reached the bottom of the stairs, Henriet's father, Prince Adolphus, came into the hall from the other side of the Palace.

"Oh, there you are, Henriet," he said, holding out his hand.

Caterina gave her friend a little push.

She ran to her father's side saying,

"I was just coming to tell you, Papa, that Caterina has arrived to join me. I know you will be pleased that she is here on such an auspicious occasion."

"I am delighted," Prince Adolphus said, holding out his hand to Caterina.

She curtseyed and, as she rose, he bent down and kissed her.

"It's so good to see you," he said. "And how is your father?"

"Very well, and very busy," she replied.

Prince Adolphus laughed.

"As we all are. I expect that you have been told by Henriet what is happening today."

"I have heard and I am very interested to see what your visitor is like. I expect he will have a great deal to tell us about what they are feeling in England at present."

He smiled.

"I am as curious as you are. We will, however, have to be very tactful in the questions we ask him."

"Yes, or course," Caterina agreed.

While she was talking to the Prince, Henriet had managed to stand a little way behind him.

As the carriage stopped outside the front door and an equerry went out, Prince Adolphus moved forward and Caterina took Henriet's hand.

She knew that her friend was trembling and her fingers tightened and then she said in a whisper that only Henriet could hear,

"Remember, dearest, how much there is at stake."

CHAPTER TWO

Caterina saw the Duke step out from the carriage and, as Prince Adolphus walked forward with outstretched hand, she could see him clearly.

He was certainly English, tall, broad-shouldered, fair-skinned and she had to admit very good-looking.

But there was definitely something about him that was intimidating, although she was not sure what it was.

He then walked into the hall and Prince Adolphus presented Henriet, who behaved beautifully.

She even forced a smile to her lips as Caterina had told her to do.

Next the Prince introduced his Lord Chamberlain and the Prime Minister and finally he came to Caterina.

"Princess Caterina," he declared, "is the daughter of Prince Otto of Theiss. She is a dear friend of my daughter and we are happy to have her with us today."

The Duke took Caterina's hand in his and, when she looked up at him, she had the strange feeling that he was questioning her.

She could not explain to herself what the feeling was, but it was definitely there.

She was anxious that, as she had implied jokingly to Henriet, he could read her thoughts.

Then Prince Adolphus was about to take the Duke away to his private apartments, when he hesitated for a moment, wondering if he should take Henriet with them.

Then he saw her glancing towards Caterina.

"We will meet later at luncheon," he said. "In the meantime I have many matters to discuss with His Grace."

Caterina was aware that Henriet heaved a sigh of relief and, taking her by the hand, drew her into the garden.

"If we want to talk," she said, "this is where we will not be overheard."

There was an ornate stone seat by the fountain and they sat down on it.

"He is frightening," Henriet murmured, "terrifying, and I cannot and will not marry him!"

"Now, dearest, you cannot judge someone you have only shaken by the hand," Caterina told her.

"I knew the moment I saw him that I hated him," Henriet insisted. "I will not marry him, whatever Papa may say. I will not! *I will not!*"

Henriet repeated the words frantically and Caterina recognised that she must soothe her.

"I have not forgotten my promise," she said. "And I have been thinking all the time about how you can avoid marrying him, but then you must play your part cleverly. If people find out what we are thinking, they would make sure that you and Fritz never met again."

Henriet was silent for a moment and then asked,

"What are you planning and how can we escape? I saw Fritz last night and he knows – we have to."

"You saw him last night?" Caterina asked her in surprise. "But how and where?"

"I am not going to tell you," Henriet said, "because it's a place that only we know where we are safe. But Fritz asked me to tell you that he is informing the General this morning that he has received news that his mother is very ill. He is therefore resigning from the Regiment and going to stay with her at the far end of the country. In fact it is miles and miles from here."

Caterina thought this a sensible move to make, but she could not help feeling that, wherever he went, Henriet would be prevented somehow from ever joining him.

They sat for a while in silence before Caterina said,

"I wanted to talk to your Fritz, so I am sorry he has gone away so far."

Henriet gave a little laugh.

"Of course he has not really gone. He merely said so and he is actually near the Palace where no one would ever expect to find him. I am meeting him again tonight, so I can tell him exactly what is happening."

"Then I must see him too," Caterina persisted. "It's even more important to find out as soon as you have talked to the Duke when your marriage is planned to take place."

"Papa must give me time, but my lady's maid told me this morning, and she always knows everything, that he has already ordered the wedding dress and there are seven seamstresses working day and night to make it for me."

"Your lady's maid always knows everything?"

"Oh, I forgot to tell you about Malca," Henriet said. "As you well know, she adores me and has been with me ever since I was a baby. I had to tell her about Fritz, for otherwise she would have had a stroke if she had found my bed empty and I was not to be seen."

Caterina naturally knew that Malca was a middle-aged woman who had been Henriet's Nanny and then when Henriet was too old to have one, Malca had refused to leave her.

"I may be trained to look after small children," she said, "but the Princess needs me and I will never leave her till I go to my grave."

25

The whole Palace had thought it very touching and so Malca had a special position in that, although she was a servant, she was allowed to do almost as she wished.

Caterina therefore knew that it was perfectly safe for Henriet to confide in her and at least if she tried to do anything drastic like committing suicide, Malca, if no one else, would be able to control her.

"If you want to meet Fritz," Henriet was saying, "Malca will take you to her room and from there you can slip out the way I do and she will tell you where he is."

"I tell you what I will do," Caterina replied. "I will say I have a headache and go to bed early, while you will doubtless have to stay in attendance on the Duke. Malca can then take me to Fritz."

"You are not to try to persuade him to stop loving me," Henriet muttered darkly.

Caterina smiled.

"I know without your telling me that it would be a waste of time. And I would never be disloyal to you."

She paused for a moment and then added,

"I want you to try to be practical, Henriet. It would save so much trouble if you could do as your father wants."

"Marry the Duke!" Henriet exclaimed and her voice rose to a scream. "*Nothing* will ever make me. Nothing! Nothing! Nothing! I expected he would look terrible and – when he stepped out of that carriage, to me it might have been the Devil himself!"

Caterina realised that she had to calm her down.

"Now listen, dearest, you are acting a part and it's always wise to act it all the time. Not just when you think people are watching you."

"I know what you are saying to me, Caterina, and I am trying to do what you tell me. Equally I am terrified that somehow you will prevent me from running away with Fritz."

"I will never do that," Caterina said, "and I promise I am trying to find a way for you to escape. But it still seems very very difficult."

It was impossible to say more because they saw an equerry coming across the lawn looking for them and, as he reached them, he bowed to Henriet and said,

"His Royal Highness requests that you to go to his sitting room."

Caterina sensed that Henriet winced and she asked,

"Can I come too? I am longing to meet the Duke."

"His Royal Highness asked only for the Princess," the equerry answered, "but if Your Highness goes with her, I suppose there is nothing he can do about it."

Caterina laughed.

"You are so right and that's what I will do. Come on, Henriet, let's do as your father wishes. As it is nearly time for luncheon, we will not have to be with him for very long."

She took Henriet's hand as she spoke and realised that her friend was now trembling.

As they started to walk across the lawn, she said in a whisper that only Henriet could hear,

"Do smile, you have to look happy as if you are looking forward to your wedding."

"I want to scream, cry and run away!"

"If you do that, it will be disastrous," Caterina said. "So be very very careful."

It was impossible to say more as they had by now reached the front door of the Palace.

The equerry was walking just ahead of them down the long passages that led to the Prince's private rooms.

As they entered, the two men were standing at the window each with a glass of champagne in his hand.

The equerry led them in, but did not announce them and Prince Adolphus turned round with a smile.

"Oh, here you are, Henriet," he began, "and I might have guessed that Caterina would be with you."

"It's lovely to have her here," Henriet murmured.

"Of course it is," her father agreed, "and I am sure Caterina will help you, as your wedding will be somewhat of a rush."

"Why should it be so hurried?" Caterina asked, as Henriet did not reply.

The Duke now spoke for the first time.

"I promised Her Majesty Queen Victoria I would not be away for long," he replied. "As I expect you know, I have come in the fastest Ironclad that the British Navy possesses and it is required on other duties more important than conveying me and my bride."

It struck Caterina that she would like to see an Ironclad, as she had been told they were more up to date than any other Battleship in the world.

But Henriet moved nearer to her father and asked.

"Must everything really be done in such a hurry, Papa? My wedding is very special for me and I have to choose my bridesmaids."

Caterina thought that she was being rather clever and she quickly added to support her,

"Of course I want to be one, Henriet."

"Then I am afraid that you are both going to be disappointed," the Prince replied. "His Grace has informed me that he wishes to leave here in two days' time, which means the marriage will have to be very simple, although, of course, it must be celebrated in the City to make our neighbours aware of its vital significance."

"I am sure you are extremely wise to make such arrangements," the Duke said. "Her Majesty, I can indeed tell you, is exceedingly shocked, in fact horrified, at the behaviour of the Russians."

"I am afraid that they have already taken over many Principalities in the Balkans," Prince Adolphus said, "and I am told that their Cossacks are creating chaos in Asia."

"The British Government has only just woken up to the realisation," the Duke said, "that they are getting nearer and nearer to India and we are therefore strengthening our forces there."

"That is sensible of you," the Prince added, "and I cannot adequately express how grateful we are in Austria that Her Majesty Queen Victoria is thinking of us too."

"I think she has always had a soft spot in her heart for this country," the Duke smiled.

Caterina was aware that Henriet's hand in hers had tightened.

"If you really intend," she said, "that the wedding should happen in two days' time, Henriet and I must start at once to buy all that she will require for her trousseau."

"It will be easy to buy anything that is necessary in London," the Duke said. "Our shops are full of delightful gowns from Paris and, as His Royal Highness knows, we have the best tailors in the world."

"But that does not really concern Henriet," Caterina pointed out. "You must appreciate that a bride wishes to look beautiful on the most important day of her life."

"I am sure the Princess could not fail to do that," the Duke answered.

It was a polite speech, but there was a slightly cynical note in his voice that Caterina did not miss.

"Nevertheless," she replied, "You must understand that Henriet feels she will want many things which every bride is entitled to require for her trousseau. Therefore we must start shopping at once. Only please tell me a little more about the wedding itself."

"I have naturally left that in the hands of His Royal Highness," the Duke said almost sharply.

Caterina turned towards the Prince and said,

"You cannot, Uncle Adolphus, be so indifferent to Henriet's needs."

She had always called him 'Uncle' when she was very young and was continually at the Palace and it had been impossible to keep stumbling over the words 'His Royal Highness'.

So he had suggested she should call him 'Uncle', which she found far easier to say.

She thought it at least put the Duke in his place and he could not in the future question anything she wanted to do with or for Henriet.

"As soon as we have finished luncheon," she said, "you must permit us to go shopping and I hope that you are feeling rich!"

Prince Adolphus laughed.

"Whatever you may buy, I feel sure that you will not bankrupt me, but I think we are doing things in a back-to-front way and I am sure that the Duke would like to talk to Henriet alone."

Henriet wanted to cry out in sheer horror, but she managed to stifle it.

Then Caterina said quickly,

"He will have to do that after the shops close. He can hardly expect poor Henriet to start married life with out of date old gowns, which will certainly not impress the English when they see them."

"Then it is off shopping you must go," the Prince conceded and his eyes were twinkling.

He knew that Caterina was very cleverly preventing Henriet from having to be alone with the Duke.

Fortunately luncheon was announced a few seconds later and they went into the dining room.

It had been the policy of the Prince since becoming a widower to have the Lord Chamberlain, equerries and other members of the Royal Household to take luncheon and dinner with him.

When he was married, he and his wife always had luncheon alone without even one Lady-in-Waiting present, but it was a routine he had no intention of continuing when his wife was no longer there.

Many people sat down at the Palace to luncheon and at dinner there were often visitors from other countries to the Capital.

When Caterina was young, she had always found the Diplomats from other countries very interesting and she enjoyed their ideas and new topics of conversation.

Today the only visitor was the Duke and so she guessed that the Prime Minister and other Officials would appear later at dinnertime.

Henriet was seated next to the Duke, who was on the Prince's right, while Caterina was on the other side of the table.

It appeared as soon as they sat down that the Prince and the Duke had a great deal to say to one another and they talked first about foreign affairs and the behaviour of the Russians.

In fact to Caterina's relief she and Henriet were hardly brought into the conversation throughout the meal.

She had been quite prepared to contribute and in fact she knew a great deal about what they were discussing.

But Henriet with downcast eyes ate very little and said nothing.

It was then a great relief when the third course was taken away and Caterina was able to say,

"Henriet and I don't need coffee. I expect, Uncle Adolphus, you and your guest will have a glass of port. So if you will excuse us we will start shopping."

The Prince agreed and they went upstairs.

When they reached Henriet's bedroom she shrieked hysterically,

"I hate him! I hate him! You saw how he was ignoring me completely and talking only to Papa. He has no interest in me and never will have! Oh, Caterina, you must save me!"

"That is what I am going to do," Caterina replied, "and that is why we came away as soon as we could."

"I would have screamed out loud if we had stayed any longer," Henriet muttered.

"Let's find out what has been planned. Neither of them talked about the actual arrangements for the wedding, although we asked them to do so."

"I don't want to hear! And I don't want to listen!"

Caterina, however, was determined to know exactly what had been arranged.

When they went downstairs, they found the Lord Chamberlain in the hall.

He was an elderly man and very charming and he smiled at the two girls.

"I can see you are off to enjoy yourselves spending money!" he began.

"It is always more enjoyable when it is not one's own money," Caterina replied.

He laughed as she drew him to one side.

"What we want to know and no one seems willing to tell us, is what exactly has been planned. It's important for Henriet, if for no one else to know what will happen."

"Of course it is," the Lord Chamberlain agreed.

"What I have been told to do now is to inform the City that the wedding will take place on Thursday morning in the Cathedral."

He smiled at her before continuing,

"A carriage will then take the bride and bridegroom to the Port where the English Battleship is waiting."

Caterina stared at the Lord Chamberlain.

"Is there to be no Reception?"

"No. The Duke is insistent that the moment he is married he must return to his duties in England."

He glanced to see that no one was listening before he added,

"If you ask me, it's rather insulting on the part of the British, but naturally I cannot say so."

"No, of course not," Caterina agreed. "But now we know, it does make it easier for Henriet than if she had to stand for hours shaking hands with people she has never even seen before."

The Lord Chamberlain laughed.

"Which is what happens to most of us on such an occasion!"

"Well, as I said," Caterina answered, "it will be easier for Henriet, although a great number of people will be disappointed not to attend a Royal Reception."

"His Royal Highness is aware of that," the Lord Chamberlain replied. "But the Duke was insistent and we therefore have to make the Service itself as impressive as possible and also give orders to the City."

"How are you doing that?" Caterina asked.

"You will see when you go shopping that I have ordered flags to be erected as quickly as possible and the Town Criers are going from street to street announcing that the wedding is to take place. So at least there will be a crowd outside the Cathedral."

"What about the country folk? They too will want to know."

"I have thought about that," the Lord Chamberlain said. "Courtiers and soldiers are already carrying the news to the Mayor of every town and I think they will celebrate locally as best they can, although, of course, they will not have much time."

He paused and then, as if to make things a little better, he said,

"After the bride and bridegroom have left, there will be fireworks and dancing in the City Square and His Royal Highness is granting every town and village some money to spend on the celebrations."

"I congratulate you. I never imagined you could start things moving so quickly."

The Lord Chamberlain now looked round to make certain that no one was listening.

"I will let you into a secret. This was planned by His Royal Highness before we had an answer from Queen Victoria. We felt certain she would not be able to refuse."

"In other words, you have been determined to have someone from England to wave the Union Jack."

"If you ask me, I think it was the Emperor's idea," the Lord Chamberlain replied. "But our Prince was always extremely enthusiastic about it."

Henriet had been listening, but she had not said a word.

"Well, thank you for all the information," Caterina said. "We will have to do our best to abide by it."

She did not wait for the Lord Chamberlain to say that there was no alternative.

She then hurried Henriet into the carriage waiting outside and, as they drove away, Henriet said,

"I am being treated like a child with no one telling me anything until the last moment."

Caterina thought the reason for that was obvious.

Her father obviously feared that she might rebel at being married to a man she did not know and who came from another country.

But there was no point in saying so and she merely replied,

"Now we have to make up our minds what we want to buy."

"I don't want anything," Henriet cried. "I can only tell you again, Caterina, that I am not going to marry that nasty horrible man. If I cannot run away with Fritz, as he wants me to, there will be a funeral and not a wedding for Papa to attend."

She was speaking hysterically, but at the same time Caterina knew that she meant every word.

They went to the shops and tried on the wedding dress, which was nearly completed.

It was very beautiful and there was a delightful lace veil to go with it and, as the seamstresses then pointed out, it would fit very comfortably under the tiara that the bride would be wearing on her head.

Caterina knew that there was a special tiara that every Royal bride of Istria wore on her wedding day.

It had been handed down for generations and, when they were much younger, she and Henriet had tried it on and laughed because they looked so Regal in it.

The design was of flowers studded with diamonds amid a number of hearts and there were diamond hearts on the wedding gown too, which Caterina thought was rather unnecessary.

One thing was quite obvious, that no one had in the least worried about the bride's heart, nor did they expect her to have any loving feelings towards her bridegroom.

'It's all very well,' Caterina thought, 'for the Prince to put his country first, but we women have to live in it!'

There was, however, no point in having ideas like this when there was so much at stake.

*

When they drove back to the Palace, she was aware that Henriet was deep in thought.

She was certain, because she knew her so well, that she was trying to plan how she could escape with Fritz or perhaps how she could kill herself.

As they neared the Palace, Caterina reminded her,

"Don't forget I am to meet your Fritz tonight."

"I have not forgotten and I want to tell him that, whatever you or Papa say, I will not wear that horrible, beastly wedding dress."

She spoke violently and Caterina said quietly,

"I know that, dearest, but be very careful and smile prettily until the moment that Fritz can carry you off. You don't want him to come under suspicion."

"No – of course not," Henriet mumbled.

"If they do discover what he is intending, they will undoubtedly arrest or even destroy him," Caterina added. "That is why you have to play your part right up to the very moment you leave."

"Leave? Do you mean that we can leave?"

"I think I have just thought of a possible way, but I must discuss it first with Fritz."

"Do you really think I shall be able to go away with him?" Henriet asked excitedly, her eyes suddenly flashing.

"I am making no promises," Caterina replied. "As I have warned you, you have to be very careful. Even this carriage may have ears! Don't let's talk of anything unless we are out of doors or somewhere we can be quite certain that no one is listening."

Henriet slipped her hand into Caterina's.

"You really are going to save me?" she asked her. "You have always helped me ever since we were children and you cannot fail me now – "

"I will not fail you if I can possibly avoid it."

"Then I am not as frightened as I was. When I saw that bridal gown, I wanted to scream and tear it to pieces."

"That would have been very silly and quite fatal."

The carriage came to a standstill outside the Palace.

And, as the two girls climbed out, they saw the Duke standing in the hall with the Prince.

"Oh, you are back!" he exclaimed. "The Duke and I are going to the Cathedral to make final plans with the Archbishop. I don't suppose you want to come with us."

"We are much too busy," Caterina replied before Henriet could speak. "It's all very well for the bridegroom, he only has to put on his best bib and tucker. But you are not giving us a reasonable time to buy a very expensive and glamorous trousseau."

"I suppose I should be grateful for that," the Prince teased.

"On the contrary, if the people have to work all night, they will charge you double," Caterina responded.

The Prince laughed at this and then the Duke said,

"I think, Your Royal Highness, that the Archbishop will be waiting for us."

"Yes, yes, of course," the Prince agreed and led the way out of the front door.

Only as they disappeared did Caterina think that the Duke was just as unpleasant as Henriet thought him to be.

'Of course no one would wish to marry a man who arranged the wedding before he had even proposed,' she reflected.

Then she recognised that the Prince was being quite clever in realising his daughter's reluctance to marry the Duke and so was keeping her apart from the bridegroom.

They would have gone up to Henriet's room, but Caterina suggested,

"Come out into the garden. The sun is shining and it's a pity not to be among the flowers."

She took Henriet by the arm and led her out into the garden.

They had not gone far before Henriet said,

"If we disappear into the shrubbery and no one is watching us, I know where we can reach Fritz."

"You do?"

"Come quickly, but look back first and see that no one is following us or watching us from the Palace."

It seemed to Caterina that the windows were empty and there was certainly no one to be seen.

Henriet led her through the shrubbery until at the far end there was a hut and it was the one they used to play in when they were children.

It was quite a large hut and the Royal Nannies had at one time kept their prams in it as well as numerous toys.

Now the door was closed and someone had put a lock on it, which Caterina did not remember.

Henriet stopped outside and looked round.

There was certainly no one to pry on them from the flower beds nor from the roses growing in great profusion above them, otherwise there were just trees and one could look over the flat land beyond the Palace and see the sea.

Henriet was opening the door of the hut with a key she had taken from her handbag.

As she went inside and Caterina followed her, she closed the door and locked it from the inside.

Caterina was intrigued, but said nothing and then to her surprise Henriet knelt down on the floor.

Pulling aside a rug, she knocked on the bare boards under it and, as she put the rug back in its place, Caterina looked at her.

"Now what happens?" she asked.

"Wait and see," Henriet replied.

She glanced towards a bare wall, which was made of wood like the rest of the hut.

Some minutes passed and both girls were silent.

Then suddenly, to Caterina's astonishment, part of the wall opened and Fritz Hofer came out.

He was not wearing his uniform but casual clothes, which somehow made him seem taller and more handsome than she remembered.

As he stepped out of the wall towards them, Henriet gave a little cry and jumped to her feet.

She flung herself against him and, looking down, he asked her very softly,

"Are you all right, my darling?"

Watching them, there was no question, Caterina thought, that he loved Henriet as much as she loved him.

It was not just the way he spoke, but how he looked and the gentle way he put his arms round her.

"I have brought Caterina to see you," Henriet said. "Things are terrible and it is all getting nearer and nearer."

"You are not to frighten yourself," Fritz Hofer said. "I had a feeling you would come to me this afternoon."

"I did not think we would have a chance, but Papa and that horrible Duke have just gone to the Cathedral."

For a moment Fritz Hofer's eyes flickered and it told Caterina more than any words could how deeply he felt about Henriet.

Then he moved forward to hold out his hand.

"Henriet tells me that you are going to help us," he said, "although I cannot reason out how it can be done."

"I have an idea," Caterina replied, "that I want you to hear. I want you to be very very honest and tell me if you think it's impossible."

"I will not only listen but I will pray that you will tell me how I can marry the only woman who I have ever loved," Fritz said, "and who I believe loves me."

"I love you, you know I love you," Henriet burst out. "As I have told you a thousand times, I would rather die than marry anyone else."

Fritz looked at Caterina.

He could not put into words what he was asking.

"I know exactly what you are both feeling," she said quietly, "and it's going to be difficult, very difficult. But somehow we have to save Henriet."

She did not have to add, 'from killing herself.' And she knew that Fritz was thinking the same as she was.

The unspoken words seemed to flash between them as if transmitted with fire.

There were chairs stacked against a wall, but Fritz and the two girls sat down on the rug. Henriet sat as close to him as she could and he put his arm round her waist to support her.

Looking at them, Caterina recognised that, if any two people were made for each other, they were and it would be wicked to part them.

She saw by the way that Henriet was looking up at Fritz that she adored him, not only with her heart but with her soul. No other man could make her feel the same and she was equally sure that Fritz loved her.

She had always thought when she had met him on other occasions that he was intelligent and she knew now that he was throwing away his career as a soldier and might even be endangering his life.

But nothing could prevent him from loving Henriet and it would be cruel to make them lead separate lives.

Yet Fate had decreed that Henriet was an essential part of the Emperor's policy to make his country more secure and she had no choice but to obey his command.

Now watching the two of them in silence Caterina realised that everything depended on her.

She alone could find a way out of the intolerable situation they found themselves in and there was no one else they could appeal to for help.

After a while Fritz asked,

"I know it seems an absurd question, but is there any way you think you could make it possible for Henriet and me to be together?"

As if he was justifying himself, he went on quickly,

"From the first moment I saw her I fell in love. I have watched her closely in the last two years grow more beautiful, more adorable and to me very very wonderful."

Henriet gave a little murmur and then hid her face against his shoulder.

"I never presumed," Fritz went on, "to offer myself as a husband for anyone so important in her own right as Henriet. Then by a miracle she loved me and I realised that I was the luckiest man in the world, at the same time the unluckiest."

"I can understand that," Caterina said. "I know that you really love each other and it would be a wicked cruelty to separate you."

"That is just what I have said over and over again," Henriet cried. "I cannot leave Fritz and go away with a man I hate to a country I have never seen. I would much rather die."

Caterina saw Fritz's arms tighten round her as if he was afraid that was what Henriet would do.

"Now listen to me," Caterina said. "I only hope and pray that, with God's help, I can save you both."

CHAPTER THREE

Before either Henriet or Fritz could say anything more there was a knock on the door.

They all three started.

With a swift movement Fritz slipped back through the opening in the wall and then disappeared, while Henriet went to the door and unlocked it.

It was with a sense of great relief that Caterina saw Malca standing there.

"His Royal Highness be lookin' for you, Princess," she said to Henriet.

Henriet turned her head towards Caterina.

"Hurry," she advised. "It would be a mistake for him to realise that we have been here."

Malca had already vanished and without saying any more Henriet ran from the hut under the trees to the far side of that part of the garden.

Then breathless, she stopped and said to Caterina, who had followed her,

"Now we will walk slowly from here to the Palace. Be careful what you say to Papa."

"I will be very careful," Caterina assured her.

She thought as she spoke that they had indeed taken a tremendous risk in seeing Fritz in the afternoon, but she could understand how useful the hut was.

No one would suspect for a moment that there was another entrance to it and she was to learn very much later that it had been built by the eldest son of a previous Prince of Istria.

He had slipped out at night to meet with 'the ladies of the town', whom he found far more attractive than those who were part of the Palace retinue. In fact, he got away with his secret meetings until he became the Ruling Prince.

Only then was the hut closed up and the passage that led from it into the outside world was, as the present Ruler thought, shut for ever.

Once the girls reached the other side of the garden, Henriet slipped her arm through Caterina's and they then walked slowly from under the trees onto the lawn.

Some way from them they saw Prince Adolphus.

"Oh, there is Papa!" Henriet exclaimed and ran towards him.

Caterina followed her more slowly.

"I have been looking for you, Henriet," he said. "I did not expect you to be so far away from the Palace."

For a moment Henriet could not think of an answer, but Caterina piped up,

"I am afraid, Uncle Adolphus, that was my fault. I was trying to spy, if you call it that, on the Duke's ship, which I am told is different from any other Battleship."

"So that is what you were up to," the Prince said. "Well, you will not see it anchored offshore."

"Why not?" Caterina asked in surprise.

"Because it is already moving up the river."

Caterina gave a little cry.

"I did not think of that."

"The Duke is bringing it as near as possible to the Cathedral," the Prince replied, "and there will be just room for it to moor in the harbour."

"Then I will be able to see it," Caterina exclaimed excitedly. "I have heard that it is very awe-inspiring."

She was thinking about how the Russians had been alarmed when the Queen had sent six Ironclads through the Dardanelles.

"I am certain of one thing," the Prince was saying, "Henriet will enjoy travelling to England in it and she will, I am sure, be the first lady to do so since it was built."

Caterina saw the expression on Henriet's face and said quickly,

"Yes, of course, it will be a great experience and something I would enjoy myself."

"Well, I am afraid there will not be time for you to inspect the ship when it arrives here. The Duke wishes to leave, as you have already heard, immediately after the ceremony in the Cathedral. It will be easy for him to do so if his ship is waiting in the harbour."

"Yes, yes, of course it will," Caterina agreed at once. "Perhaps I will be able to see it another time."

She knew by the expression on Henriet's face that even to speak about the wedding and what would happen after it was making her tremble.

She therefore asked,

"Why did you want Henriet, Uncle Adolphus?"

"It's the Duke who wishes to see her. He wants to make certain that the wedding ring fits her finger."

Henriet gave a gasp and Caterina pressed her arm to warn her to be careful.

"The Duke was telling me about a friend of his to whom he was Best Man. The wedding ring did not fit and everyone claimed that it was a bad omen. Sure enough the bridegroom was then killed the following year when he fell at a steeplechase and his horse rolled on him."

"I have always thought that the English were not a superstitious people," Caterina remarked. "But perhaps the Duke is an exception."

"Well, apparently he is. Though a good horseman, he has no wish to be thrown in a steeplechase or any other sort of race!"

"No, of course not," Caterina laughed. "If he has a collection of rings for Henriet to try on, can I come and see them too."

"I would suppose so," the Prince replied. "Are you thinking of getting married?"

Caterina laughed.

"No Duke has asked for my hand yet and I doubt if I will ever have such a distinguished suitor as Henriet."

"There is plenty of time," the Prince said lightly. "I am sure that, if your father gives a ball for you, a great number of gentlemen will find you as attractive and as lovely as your mother was."

"That is a very kind thing to say, Uncle Adolphus."

She was talking away to distract his attention from Henriet, who was obviously terrified at meeting the Duke and was shrinking at the idea of trying on a wedding ring.

When they reached the Palace, the Prince stopped for a moment to speak to one of the equerries.

Caterina whispered in Henriet's ear,

"Now be calm. Don't let him suspect for a moment that you don't wish to marry the Duke or they might in some strange way attribute it to Fritz."

At the mention of his name, Henriet pulled herself together and then she said,

"I will do my best, but don't leave me – please."

"I will come with you," Caterina said, "and I will take you away as soon as I can."

She spoke confidently, but she was frightened that Henriet, who was always so emotional, would lose control of herself.

If she made the Duke aware that she had no wish to marry him and in fact hated him, anything might happen.

The Prince led them to his private sitting room.

When they went in, the Duke was standing looking out of the window and there was no one else in the room.

"I am sorry we kept you so long," the Prince said. "My daughter was in the garden looking out to see your magnificent warship. As I told her, it is coming up river where she will be able to see it closely."

He was talking to the Duke, who was looking at Henriet in a somewhat critical manner.

Caterina thought it was offensive and to divert his attention she remarked,

"My uncle has been relating how superstitious you are about wedding rings. In fact there are a great number of superstitions in this country, but I have not heard of that one before."

"Superstition or no superstition," the Duke said, "I think it would be embarrassing if the ring did not fit the bride's finger and I had to struggle to get it into place."

Caterina laughed.

"It would certainly be unusual, but, as all weddings are much the same, it might give people something new to talk about."

"They will have plenty for everybody to talk about at this wedding," the Prince said sharply, as if he thought that she was being insulting to the Duke. "And I am quite certain it will annoy the Russians and the Germans that the Queen of Great Britain is giving her protection to Istria."

"Indeed they will talk about it and will be very envious," Caterina said.

While she was speaking, the Duke had moved to a table near the fireplace and there was a large jewel-box on it which he opened.

Inside it Caterina could see several gold wedding rings and there was a very attractive necklace of pearls and diamonds.

"Which would you like first?" the Duke asked, "a present from your bridegroom or your wedding ring?"

Caterina sensed that Henriet was about to reply, 'neither!' so, before her friend could speak, she cried out,

"Oh, what a lovely necklace! It's quite the prettiest I have ever seen."

"I thought it would enhance the bride's appearance when she entered the Cathedral tomorrow and would be a gift she would be pleased to have," the Duke said rather pompously.

"It's lovely, perfectly lovely!" Caterina exclaimed, as Henriet did not speak.

She was standing looking down at it on the table, her head so low that the Duke could not see the expression in her eyes, but Caterina knew only too well exactly what she was feeling.

She picked up the necklace before the Duke could prevent her and suggested,

"Oh, Henriet, do put it on. It's so lovely and will look marvellous on your wedding dress."

She put it round her friend's neck as she spoke and fastened it at the back, then stepped back and cried,

"Oh, it's beautiful! You look absolutely lovely! It will add to the beauty of your wedding gown! It's clever of the Duke to have thought of such a marvellous present."

And it was with the greatest difficulty that Henriet managed to say,

"It's very pretty, thank you!"

As if he realised that his daughter was suffering in some way, the Prince said quickly,

"Now let's try on the wedding rings and then the Duke and I have a great many matters to discuss."

"And we have things to do too," Caterina said.

The Duke drew one of the rings from the box and Henriet put out her hand.

It was trembling so much that Caterina took hold of her arm and put her other hand on her wrist.

The Duke slipped the ring onto Henriet's finger, but it would not pass over the knuckle.

"It's too small," Caterina said. "Suppose I try one of the rings for her. Henriet and I have always exchanged our jewellery and I often forget which is hers and which is mine. I had a sapphire ring which Henriet refuses to give back to me because it fits her so well and goes with a pair of her earrings!"

The Duke laughed.

"I have a feeling I will have to give both of you rings for Christmas presents. I had no idea that you were sharing them."

"They are in rather short supply," Caterina said. "Papa will not part with the ones that belonged to Mama and the most valuable of Henriet's mother's jewellery is locked away in the safe."

"It's certainly a sad story," the Prince commented.

While he was speaking, Caterina had held out her left hand to the Duke and he slipped on another ring which was larger than the first. It was of plain gold and she thought rather ugly, but it fitted her.

"That will, of course, fit Henriet. Do you want to try it on, dearest?" she asked.

"If it fits you – it fits me," Henriet managed to say.

But there was a slight break in her voice that made Caterina say quickly,

"Now we must go! We have a dressmaker waiting for us upstairs and I am sure that the longer she has to wait the more expensive the gown will become."

"It would not surprise me at all," the Prince said.

Caterina, holding Henriet by the hand, had already reached the door.

Only as she did so, did she realise that the beautiful pearl and diamond necklace was still round her neck.

"Shall Henriet keep the necklace," she asked the Duke, "to wear tomorrow? Or do you want it back?"

"No, of course not. It is a family heirloom and I brought it for my future wife to wear on our wedding day. It certainly looks very becoming."

"Then, of course, she will be thrilled to wear it."

Caterina had kept on talking since she realised that Henriet was past saying anything.

She pulled her through the door and shut it quickly behind them.

Then without another word the two girls ran down the passage and up the stairs to Henriet's bedroom.

Only when they were inside the room and the door was closed did Henriet explode,

"I hate him! I hate him! I don't want his horrible necklace or his ring."

She pulled off the necklace as she spoke and flung it on the bed and then she burst into tears.

"I hate him! I hate him!" she sobbed. "I will kill myself rather than marry him and neither you nor anyone else can stop me!"

Caterina put her arms round her and she went on sobbing until at last Caterina said soothingly,

"You have to be sensible, dearest."

"You said – you would save me, but now he has – a wedding ring and I cannot escape. I know there is no way I can."

The words came almost incoherently from her and she was shaking as she wept against Caterina's shoulder.

Then Caterina said rather sharply,

"Listen, dearest Henriet, I have promised to save you and I will do so. But you have to promise me that you will do nothing desperate until I have it clearly in my mind what will happen."

"What *can* happen?" Henriet cried. "Except that I will have to marry that dreadful man when I want to stay here and be with Fritz."

Caterina realised it was hopeless to reason with her.

"Please, please try to stop crying and listen to me, Henriet."

"I am not going to listen to you anymore," Henriet sobbed. "I have a revolver of Papa's. He was teaching me to shoot with it. But now I am going to use it on myself."

Caterina stiffened.

She had not appreciated that things had gone so far or that Henriet had a weapon that she could use to actually destroy herself.

She now asserted firmly,

"Stop crying and I will tell you what we are going to do."

"I am not going to listen," Henriet wept. "You are going to tell me – I must think about Istria and not myself. But I hate not only the Duke – but Papa and the Emperor for choosing me when there are hundreds of other women who would be only too pleased – to be a heroine of their own country."

Her words were almost incoherent, but they told Caterina that she had lost control and it would be hopeless to try to make her understand anything.

She held her close, kissed her cheek and then said,

"Now I am going back to see if Fritz is still there and suggest to him a way you can escape together."

Henriet was suddenly still.

"Did you say – escape together?" she asked.

"That is what I said," Caterina answered. "I think I have a way, but I must talk to Fritz first."

"Then I am sure he will be there and can I not come with you?"

"No, that would be a mistake. Your father might want you again and would think it strange that you have rushed back into the garden. If we put the plan I have in my mind into operation, we must not make any false step."

Henriet understood this and moved from Caterina's arms and started to wipe her eyes.

"Have you *really* an idea of how you can save me?" she asked.

"I promise you I have, but, as I said, I must speak to Fritz first. If anyone asks where I am, say you think I have gone to my bedroom. And so you must stay here. Do you promise, Henriet?"

"I – promise."

Caterina held out her hand.

"Give me the revolver," she ordered.

"No, I want to – keep it," Henriet replied. "If you cannot save me, I will use it tomorrow before I have – to go to the Cathedral."

She spoke in a way that made Caterina realise she was indeed serious, very serious! And it was no use trying to persuade her to be anything else.

"Actually I believed that you trusted me," Caterina said. "I need the revolver for Fritz in case he does not have one."

"To protect himself – and me?" Henriet questioned.

"That was my idea," Caterina replied.

"Then, of course, if Fritz wants it, he must have it."

Henriet went over to her dressing table and opened a drawer. At the back of it there was a secret place for which she had a key.

She took out what Caterina realised was a very up to date and expensive revolver.

Because she looked at it in surprise, Henriet said,

"Papa thought someone had stolen it, but I have had it here ever since he told me I had to marry the Duke."

"I will give it to Fritz," Caterina said. "It will be safer with him than with you."

She bent and kissed her friend.

"Now be very careful," she cautioned, "that no one is at all suspicious as to where I have gone and why we are not together."

She smiled before she added,

"I will be back as quickly as I can. But I am just praying that Fritz will have stayed in the hut in case you returned."

"Tell him I wanted to, but you would not let me."

"He will surely understand, especially when I tell him what my plan is."

Caterina kissed Henriet again and then she slipped out of the door, hoping that there would be no servants on the landing.

To her relief there was no one and so she hurried towards the backstairs that Henriet had always taken when she went out into the garden to see Fritz.

They led to a side door that was not often used.

The servants slept in a different part of the Palace and only Malca slept near Henriet amongst the bedrooms which were allocated to guests.

The door led directly to a mass of rhododendron bushes and olive trees and moving amongst them she knew that she could not be seen by anyone in the Palace.

Then she reached the end of the garden and the hut where they had been with Fritz.

She had picked up the key that Henriet kept in her dressing table drawer while she was finding the revolver, which Caterina was now carrying in her hand.

She opened the door of the hut and locked herself in, just as Henriet had done previously.

Then she pulled back the rug and knocked on the floor.

As she did so, she was praying that Fritz would not have left and gone back to his Regiment.

It was with immense relief when the secret panel in the wall opened and Fritz peeped out.

He looked at Caterina and then came into the hut.

"Where is Henriet?" he asked. "And did her father suspect that she was down here?"

"No, he had no idea," Caterina replied. "We had reached the other side of the garden before he saw us. I told

54

him that I had been looking for the Duke's Ironclad, which I understand is now in the river."

Fritz drew in his breath and she saw that there was an expression of despair in his eyes.

Caterina sat down on the floor.

"Now, listen to me," she said. "I need your brains, otherwise what I am going to propose will be a disaster."

"What are you suggesting?" Fritz asked nervously.

He sat down beside her and she thought how good-looking he was. Even in the rough ordinary clothes he was disguised in, there was no mistaking that he was a man of quality and good breeding.

"First of all I brought this," Caterina said, handing him the revolver. "It's what Henriet intended to kill herself with if she was forced to marry the Duke."

"Just how could she think of anything so wicked?" Fritz sighed. "She is so young, she is so beautiful and she will forget me."

Caterina smiled.

"I think that would be impossible. Although I did not credit it at first, I do now believe her when she says that she would rather die than marry anyone but you."

Fritz's lips tightened and there was a pain in his eyes which was unmistakable.

However, he took the revolver from Caterina and put it in the pocket of his coat.

"What can I do?" he asked.

"I thought of this plan before, but hoped it would not be necessary. Now, however, I know the only way of saving Henriet is *for me to take her place*."

Fritz stared at her.

"What on earth do you mean?"

"Exactly what I say. I love Henriet and I am now absolutely convinced in my own mind that she will destroy herself rather than marry the Duke when she is so much in love with you."

She paused a moment before she continued,

"I have taken the revolver away from her, but there is nothing to stop her jumping off the roof of the Palace or finding some other weapon."

Fritz was silent and Caterina knew that there were no words he could use to express what he was feeling.

"So we have to be very clever. No one must have the slightest suspicion until I am actually married to the Duke that he is not marrying the daughter of the Prince of Istria."

"How can you do that?" Fritz asked. "It's too big a decision for any girl of your age to take."

"It is simply a question of my suffering or Henriet dying. Because I love her and she has always been a sister to me, I cannot take the risk that she might destroy herself, if not before the wedding, then immediately after it."

"I must talk to her," Fritz asserted.

"What can you say except that, whilst you love her and will never love anyone else, you can sadly never be together?"

There was silence and then Fritz enquired,

"Is there anything I can do to prevent this marriage taking place?"

Caterina smiled and she knew that he was really asking how he could kill himself.

"That is easy to answer. You must take Henriet away before I marry the Duke. And no one must have the slightest suspicion it has happened until we have left the country and are on our way to England."

Fritz bent forward and took her hand in his and raised it to his lips.

"I never knew that any woman would sacrifice herself for another in such a magnificent manner."

"We only have a little time to arrange everything. You have to take Henriet away and out of the country the moment we have arranged for her to meet you."

It was then she understood just why Fritz Hofer was recognised to be a very good soldier.

Instead of continuing to talk about the sacrifice she was making, he said,

"I have a yacht. I could send it not up the river, where it would be seen, but to wait just a little way down the coast. It will not be hard to reach, as it would be less than three miles from here."

"How will you go to it?" Caterina enquired.

"It would be best if Henriet could meet me here tonight when everyone is asleep. Then we can be some way out to sea before dawn. If you are taking her place, it will be up to you to make sure that no one in the Palace knows you are the bride instead of Henriet."

"That is what I thought. And the only person we can trust to help us is Malca."

"She adores Henriet," he said, "and has been deeply depressed that 'her baby' has to marry a man she has not met until now and is of a different nationality to her own."

"Of course we all realise that, but I feel I will be able to cope with it better than Henriet could."

"She is such a child in so many ways," Fritz said. "That is one reason why I love her. I want to make certain that she never suffers again as she is suffering now."

"I am sure you will both be very very happy," she replied. "I would certainly not sacrifice myself, as you call it, if I was not sure of that."

Fritz was thinking.

"What I will do," he said, "is to come to the hut and collect Henriet at one o'clock in the morning."

Caterina nodded.

"You must take her away and I will send Malca after you later, although, of course, I will need her now to keep everyone out of Henriet's room and to help me while I am dressing tomorrow."

They were both aware as she spoke that this was very dangerous.

If anyone in the Palace had the slightest idea that Henriet was running away with him, his yacht would be followed by every ship the Prince possessed. They might even send the British Battleship after them, in which case they would have no possible chance of disappearing.

"What I must do," Caterina said, "is to take Malca with me, as Henriet intended to do. She can slip off at our first Port of call. Then you could arrange to pick her up yourself or for her to travel to where you are. I will see that she has enough money."

She was thinking as she spoke that by that time the Duke would be aware that the woman he had married was not the one who had been chosen by Queen Victoria and the Emperor to be his wife.

He would undoubtedly be very angry, but there would be nothing he could do about it.

Except, she hoped, make the best of a bad job of it!

It was however, frightening to think how furious he would be.

Therefore she must concentrate now on Henriet and not think about herself.

"I am sleeping on my yacht at the moment," Fritz said, "while I am supposed to be with my mother hundreds of miles away."

He thought for a moment and then said,

"I can easily move my yacht now from where it is to another cove. The only thing you have to do is to bring Henriet to me here."

"I have a feeling," Caterina said, "that the Prince has increased the guard round the Palace since the Duke arrived."

She saw the anxiety in Fritz's eyes and added,

"Not only to impress him, but to make sure when the wedding is announced that there are no inquisitive trespassers peeping through the windows or hoping for the bridegroom's autograph."

Fritz laughed as if he could not help it.

"That is one thing they will not receive!"

"They can always try and that is why I have seen more sentries than usual round the Palace at night."

"Henriet must be careful to avoid them and by one o'clock in the morning even the best of sentries begin to feel sleepy."

Caterina smiled.

"That's true, I have seen them half asleep with their heads nodding over their muskets."

"Well, let's hope they will do so tonight. And tell Henriet I will be here at exactly one o'clock."

"I will tell her and I know she will be radiantly happy."

"I just don't know what to say to you. You have been so wonderful that there are no words to express my gratitude or what I know will be Henriet's gratitude too, once she is my wife."

"Where will you go?" Caterina asked him.

"The world is a big place and I have many interests in different countries. I will miss my house here and the estate which has been in my family's possession for many generations."

"Of course you will."

"But one day," Fritz went on, "I feel sure we will come back to it. Our children will learn how fantastic it is to be an Austrian in what I consider the most attractive country in the whole of Europe."

Caterina smiled at him.

"That is exactly what I feel as well," she agreed.

"Equally I have interests in other countries, India for one and Japan for another. I think Henriet will enjoy travelling with me."

"I am sure that she will love every moment of it. No one for her really exists in the world except you and if she is thrown away on an Englishman, who I think cares for no one but himself, it will be an unforgivable crime."

"But that is what you are undertaking yourself – "

"I know, but I am not in love with someone else as Henriet is and perhaps, when I least expect it, I will find some compensation for that in England."

"There is nothing more I can say, except that I think you are marvellous. I have never known a woman so brave or so unselfish."

"I had better go back," Caterina said, rising to her feet. "I know when I tell Henriet what is arranged she will be so happy and so wildly excited it will be difficult for her to hide it."

"Don't let her go down to dinner with her future bridegroom," Fritz suggested.

"I was thinking of that and she had better have a headache. It is, of course, what every bride is entitled to have before she is married."

"You are very sensible, Caterina, and I will thank you all my life for making me the happiest man in the whole world."

"I am sure that is what you will be. So, however difficult things may be for me, it will be worthwhile."

"Go back now," he said, "and don't be seen if you can help it. I have a great deal to do before I can be back here at one o'clock."

"You must not be seen either."

"I will make sure of that. In fact, if you saw me in the disguise I wear to come here, you would not give me a second glance."

"All the same be very careful."

"I will, because I will be thinking of Henriet with all my heart."

Fritz opened the door and she slipped through it.

She then smiled at him and hurried away amongst the rhododendrons.

When she reached the Palace, she opened the door that she had left unlocked and hurried up the stairs.

As she rushed into Henriet's bedroom, she saw that she was lying on the bed with Malca beside her.

When she saw Caterina, Henriet sat up at once.

"Oh, you are back! What has happened?"

Caterina shut the door very quietly then went across the room.

Malca would have given her a chair, but instead she sat down on the bed.

"Now listen," she began in a low voice. "I have arranged everything and it all depends on you, Henriet, and Malca too, whether we are successful or we fail dismally."

Henriet drew in her breath.

"What have you arranged? Oh, darling Caterina, have you seen Fritz."

"Yes, he was there and has agreed to everything."

She paused, looked round and lowered her voice even more before she added,

"He will collect you tonight at the hut in the garden at one o'clock."

"And I am to go with him?" Henriet gasped. "Oh, Caterina, that is so wonderful! But surely Papa will send soldiers after us."

"Your father will not have the slightest idea you have gone until after you are married to Fritz." Caterina said. "No one else will know until the Duke sees me face to face on his Battleship."

"But how, just how are we to do it?" Malca asked before Henriet could speak.

"*I* will marry the Duke in your place."

Henriet gave a cry.

"You cannot do that, you cannot marry that terrible man!"

"It's a question of you or me," Caterina replied. "We have to give you time to escape."

Henriet threw herself against her friend.

"Oh, darling, darling Caterina how could you do anything so wonderful? As you know I will die if I cannot marry Fritz, but I never dreamt that you would have to take my place."

"It's the only way you can marry Fritz as you want to. I expect, although he did not tell me so, you will be married on board his yacht by the Captain, which is, of course, completely legal."

Henriet's eyes were shining.

She looked so completely different from the dismal girl Caterina had left sobbing.

"Now what you have to do is to be ready at the hut at one o'clock, when we hope everyone in the Palace will be asleep."

She paused a moment and then went on,

"Malca will let you out through the side door and Fritz will be waiting for you in the hut to take you to his yacht, which will be in a cove a little way along the coast.

Henriet was listening wide-eyed.

"You have to leave everything else in my hands. It will not be until we are finally married and safely on the Battleship and, I hope, some way out to sea that the Duke will realise what has happened."

"How can you possibly be so kind and unselfish?" Henriet asked.

"That is more or less what Fritz said. I told him that I love you like a sister and could not bear you to be unhappy. I am not in love with anyone and never have been, so I daresay I can manage the Duke, although I admit he is rather frightening."

"Oh, darling Caterina! I will be thinking of you and praying for you. Perhaps you will be able to run away from him."

"Perhaps and then perhaps not. I can only hope that it will turn out better for me than seems likely at this very moment. But what we are definitely doing is to make it better for you, dearest Henriet."

"So marvellous and so perfect that I feel as if I am flying up into the sky and touching the stars. I love Fritz and I know he loves me. It is difficult to think of anything else, except that you have given him to me and I can never, never thank you enough."

"We must not speak too soon," Caterina warned. "There are a number of pitfalls for both of us before we are really safe."

"That be true," Malca came in.

She had not spoken for some minutes and then she went on,

"We can only pray to the good Lord and hope He will protect us."

She crossed herself as she spoke.

Caterina also sent up a little prayer to Heaven that God would help them.

CHAPTER FOUR

Malca was already starting to pack the essentials for Henriet.

"What I will do," she said, "is to bring everythin' you will want when I comes to you. You will just have to manage with a few things until we are together again."

Caterina looked at Henriet.

"I feel awful," she said, "keeping Malca from you, even if only temporarily."

"Don't worry about that. I quite understand that you must have her with you until the wedding is over. I shall manage all right, but I shall feel a little lost without her until she can rejoin me."

Malca smiled at the compliment and then she said,

"Now don't be too pleased about everythin' until you are quite certain you are safe and out of reach, but how are you goin' to get in touch with me when I leave the Battleship at the first Port of call?"

"I am sure that Fritz will have a way of letting you know where we are and you must be careful to take the address from him before we leave."

"I know one thing for sure," Malca said, "you will need lookin' after even if you're married to the best man in the world and no one can do it better than I do."

"Of course not," Henriet agreed. "I have always depended on you ever since I was born and I shall look forward to you coming to me and Fritz as soon as you can."

"Now come along and be sensible," Caterina urged. "See what Malca is packing and please leave me something to wear until I can buy myself a trousseau. It's so lucky we can wear the same clothes."

"You are a little slimmer than I am, but I am sure Malca could do a few alterations on the Battleship."

"I suppose that'll be two or three days," Malca said, "and I can do quite a lot in that time, as you well know."

"Of course you can, but you must pack all Henriet's prettiest clothes for her to wear on her honeymoon."

She thought that it would indeed be her honeymoon as well, but it would not matter what she wore.

She was sure that the Duke would be extremely angry with her and even if he did not throw her overboard, perhaps they would separate before they reached England.

Then she wondered what would be his position if he arrived with the wrong girl. If nothing else, he would certainly be a laughing-stock to his friends.

Then she shrugged her shoulders.

'I cannot help his troubles,' she thought. 'And he has certainly not made himself at all agreeable since he has been here.'

Malca was packing and concentrating on what she was doing so that it was impossible to talk to her.

Henriet then drew Caterina to one side and asked,

"Tell me, darling, what will you do if the Duke makes a terrible scene and refuses to speak to you?"

"He may make a scene with me, but I am thinking that he will look very foolish when he arrives in England! He will have to think of some reasonable explanation for having married me!"

"I expect the Queen will be very very angry."

Caterina thought that the Emperor would be furious too and that might affect her father.

But there was nothing she could do now and talking about it could not make her situation any better.

She therefore went to her own bedroom where the wedding dress had just been delivered.

It was certainly the prettiest wedding dress she had ever seen and she mused that if she was wearing it any man she married would admire her.

With, of course, the exception of the Duke!

She walked over to the window and thought rather wistfully that it would be very exciting if she was getting married to someone she loved and this was the night before they were to be together.

She had often dreamt that one day she would meet a tall handsome man and they would fall in love at first sight and their marriage would be approved of by both families.

The wedding would be a moment in their lives that they would both always remember.

Instead of which, she knew, if she was honest, that she was extremely frightened of what would happen when the Duke realised that he had been deceived.

She felt a little shiver run through her and it was a relief when Malca came into the room.

"I thinks while I was packin'," she said, "it would be a good idea if I made your veil thicker than it is at the moment for your drive to the Cathedral."

"What a good idea," Caterina exclaimed. "How clever of you!"

"I've some soft tulle which will completely obscure your face, although you'll be able to see through it. You must be careful when you lifts up your veil at the end of the Service that the Duke doesn't denounce you then and there as an imposter."

For a moment Caterina shuddered and said,

"We must be incredibly silly, Malca, if we cannot deceive everyone while I am wearing the wedding veil. What I think we should do is to warn Uncle Adolphus that I am very hysterical at having to leave home and him."

"Yes, of course, Princess. If you're cryin', His Royal Highness'll find it difficult to kiss you, let alone realise you're not Henriet."

"I have often thought myself a good actress when we have performed special plays at Christmas," Caterina said. "Do you remember those we did one year to amuse Uncle Adolphus and his friends?"

"They thought you and Henriet were brilliant in the parts you played," Malca said loyally.

"Well, I must do even better tomorrow. I think the first thing is for you to tell His Royal Highness that I am very hysterical and that, if anything upsets me or if he is too affectionate, I will run away."

Malca, who was very intelligent, nodded her head.

"I've been downstairs to the Lord Chamberlain," she said, "with the excuse that I wanted to know exactly what be goin' to happen."

She paused a moment, then carried on,

"I think it'll be safest if I meet you on the ship when you arrive after the Service and take you quickly to your cabin since you're on the verge of breakin' down."

"That's a splendid idea," Caterina agreed. "I had not thought of it."

"I'll tell His Royal Highness that you might create a big scene at the last moment because you love him and hate goin' away to another country."

Caterina nodded, as this was a ploy she had actually thought of herself, but had not had time to suggest it.

"As soon as you comes aboard, I'll whisk you away into your cabin and, if I can, prevent the Duke from comin' to see you."

"That will give us time to be well out to sea and it will be impossible, now that we are actually married, for him to turn round and bring me back."

Malca smiled.

"I'll see to your veil," she said, "then I must go back to 'my baby'. She's worryin' over you, but you're savin' her from a worse fate than worryin', thank God!"

There was no need for Caterina to reply. Malca had gone closing the door firmly behind her.

She walked to the window and looked out. The sun was still shining, but the shadows were growing longer.

'Tomorrow, at this time,' she thought, 'I will be on the high seas with the Duke, waiting as if in a terrifying nightmare for him to discover that he has been hoaxed.'

Then she tried to tell herself that she would not be intimidated by him.

After all, it was he who had behaved badly in the first place.

He had come here from England, admittedly at the request of the Emperor, but had made no effort to ingratiate himself with his future bride.

In fact, she thought, he had seemed offensively cold and reserved and he was almost deliberately rude to his bride-to-be and it was no wonder that someone as soft and gentle as Henriet had disliked him from the first.

She had known that it was just unthinkable for her to become his wife.

'It's unthinkable for me as well,' Caterina thought. 'But I have to save Henriet and there is no other way.'

She thought again how she had always imagined that one day she would love someone who loved her and they would be as happy as her father and mother had been.

She could remember all too clearly the excitement in her mother's eyes and the smile on her lips when her father came home from riding or shooting and she would run into the hall to greet him.

"You are back!" she would exclaim. "Oh, darling, did you have a good day and did you enjoy yourself?"

"I would have enjoyed myself more if you had been with me," Caterina would hear her father say.

He would kiss his wife gently and then, with his arm around her, they would walk into the sitting room.

Because they were so happy and so much in love they seemed to fill the whole Palace with their joy.

Caterina knew that she had been brought up in an atmosphere of love and this was a treasure she would not know again.

She wondered if her mother would disapprove of what she was doing and she had a feeling that, because it was the only possible course open to her to save Henriet, her mother, if no one else, would understand.

It was time to dress for dinner and she went to Henriet's room to see what she was doing.

She found, and was not particularly surprised, that Malca had put her to bed and she was fast asleep.

When Malca saw Caterina, she whispered,

"If Henriet went down to dinner, I've a feelin' she'd be upsettin' herself quite unnecessarily. She'll have all the excitement she can cope with later when I take her out of the house and she has to walk to the hut without bein' seen."

Caterina knew that this sensible, but she had looked forward to being with Henriet until the last moment.

"I'm not goin' to wake her," Malca said, "until I have to or she wakes herself. So you go downstairs and tell His Royal Highness she's already in a state at havin' to leave home and him."

"You are quite right and that is very clever of you, Malca. At the same time I hate leaving Henriet and I will want to say goodbye to her."

"Of course you will and all you have to say is that you wants to go to bed early as tomorrow'll be such a strain and no one'll be surprised."

Caterina smiled at her.

"You are quite right and His Royal Highness will know that, if Henriet is in a hysterical mood, she will cling to me, just as she will cling to you."

"That's right," Malca agreed, "and if that doesn't pull the wool over his eyes, nothin' will."

Caterina laughed, but she knew that dinner was going to be somewhat uncomfortable.

Actually it was not too difficult. The Prince had thought it right that a large number of important people in the Government should meet the Duke before he left.

The conversation over dinner was mostly political and a condemnation of the way Russia was behaving.

Most of the guests brought their wedding presents with them and Caterina exclaimed with delight at every one and thanked them on behalf of Henriet.

"She will be very thrilled tomorrow when she sees them," she said, "and, of course, they will all be put aboard the Duke's ship. And they will certainly give her immense pleasure when she will naturally be a little upset at having to leave home."

"I am very sorry for the poor child," the Prime Minister's wife said. "After all she has never been to

England and she knows very few English people and I am told that everyone is scared of Queen Victoria."

"I have heard that too," Caterina replied. "But the Duke is one of Her Majesty's special favourites and she will, I am certain, be kind and understanding to Henriet."

"Well, all I can say," the Prime Minister's wife added, "is that I am very glad I am not Royal. I married my husband because he loved me and I find myself loving him more year after year. It is how a marriage should be."

Caterina agreed with her, but she could not help thinking that the Duke would be a difficult man to love.

Of one thing she was absolutely certain, after she had deceived him, that he would never love her.

As usual at the more formal dinner parties given at the Palace, this one seemed to drag slowly on until it was time for the visitors to leave.

They were particularly polite to the Duke and each one told him how happy they were that their country had this vital tie with Britain and his marriage would certainly strengthen the connection and it would make it much more difficult for Russia to interfere in their affairs.

The Duke made a short speech at the dinner table.

He said how honoured he had been to come to Istria and how touched he was by the kindness he had received.

He was taking home the picture of a people who were living happily and contentedly in a country that was growing more prosperous year by year.

"We can only be sorry for your neighbours who have a different story to tell," he said, "and I hope that in the future they will be strong enough to resist all their enemies. Of course any infringement of their independence is frowned upon by Her Majesty Queen Victoria."

His speech was loudly applauded, but Caterina felt that it was of little consolation to the Balkan Principalities that had already been gobbled up by the Russians.

She could see, however, that Prince Adolphus was delighted with the Duke's words and congratulated him warmly when he sat down.

Then he made a speech saying how honoured they were by the Duke's visit and how thrilled and delighted he was to be closer to England than he had ever been before, as his daughter would now be the Duchess of Dunlerton.

"I only regret," he said, "that my daughter is not with us this evening. You will understand that she has a long voyage in front of her and the ceremony of marriage tomorrow will be quite a strain on such a young bride."

He paused and then went on,

"However, she sends you her best wishes and will, I know, be extremely grateful for all the delightful gifts you have brought her."

He finished by saying,

"I know you will all raise your glasses and drink with me a special toast to the bride and bridegroom and wish them every happiness in their future life together."

There was a murmur of applause and everyone's glass was raised.

Caterina put her glass to her lips but did not drink, thinking that it would be unlucky to drink her own toast.

She also wondered what these people would think when they learnt, as they would sooner or later, that they had been deceived and the bride did not come from Istria but Theiss!

It was a great relief when people started to leave.

As the last guest departed Caterina said goodnight to the Prince.

"You made a marvellous speech, Uncle Adolphus," she said. "I will tell Henriet in the morning how pleased everyone was."

She could not help glancing at the Duke, who was saying nothing and she thought that he was as relieved as she was that dinner was at an end.

She therefore kissed Prince Adolphus and curtseyed to the Duke and then walked out of the reception room and up the stairs.

When she reached Henriet's room, she was a little surprised to find that she was already up and dressed.

She was wearing warm clothes, as, although it was summer, it would still be pretty chilly when the sea breezes blew over the lowland on her way to the yacht.

"You are ready!" Caterina exclaimed.

"I was awake and Malca says that there is no one in the garden so she has taken my suitcase down to the hut."

"Was that safe?"

Henriet laughed.

"Of course it was. You know Malca would never take a risk. And apparently the sentries are drinking your health this evening and enjoying themselves."

"I see the point and when are you leaving?"

"As soon as I possibly can. Fritz said he would be in the hut at one o'clock, but I expect he will be earlier. It would be more dangerous when the moon is fully up and someone might see us walking to the sea."

Caterina felt that that this was sensible.

If they were just a couple strolling around in the moonlight, no one would give them a second thought, but, if they were carrying heavy suitcases, it would be natural to wonder why and where they were going.

It meant a lot of walking for Fritz. At the same time he was a strong, athletic man, who one would not expect to sit cooped up in a hut for any length of time.

"So you will be leaving, Henriet, as soon as Malca thinks it is safe."

"If I have to wait in the hut, it will not matter, but if I wait here, there is always the possibility that someone might burst in on me."

"Malca must lock the door as soon as you have gone," Caterina suggested.

"You will have to do that," Henriet replied, "while Malca comes with me to the hut. She thought it would be a mistake if you took me, as I would have liked you to do."

She put her hand in Caterina's.

"If we are by any chance stopped by a sentry," she went on, "we can simply say that we wanted some fresh air because it was hot and we are just walking in the garden."

"I can see you have thought of everything."

She could not help thinking that, because Henriet was so in love, she was using her brain far more than she usually did.

She was used to people pandering to her, cosseting her and, of course, loving her, but she was their Princess and there had never been any need for her to think for herself, but now she was doing so, it was certainly a step in the right direction.

"Now before you go, Henriet, I must get you to tell me how I can communicate with you, just in case anything goes wrong."

"Fritz has thought of that already. He has written down the place we are going to, where you can either write or send a telegram."

She handed a sheet of paper to Caterina, who put it quickly down the front of her evening gown.

"No one will see it," she said. "But, now I have it, I feel safer for you and later for Malca."

"I have given Malca a copy of the same list and the address of some friends of Fritz's who will always know where we are. I have given her plenty of money so that she can sail to wherever we are or where we will be calling in."

"I see you have thought of everything," Caterina said again, "and it's certainly very clever of you and Fritz. Now all I have to do is to pretend to be you until we are out at sea."

Henriet then impulsively threw her arms round her friend's neck.

"I want to thank you again and again for being so wonderful," she sighed. "But there are no words left."

"I don't want to hear them," Caterina said. "All I want to know is that you and Fritz will be happy for ever. I am certain that, once he is over the shock, your father will want you to come back here."

Henriet thought for a moment.

"Of course I will mind leaving Papa and I will be longing to see him again. But it depends if he forgives me and Fritz or not."

"I am sure he will, but he will be angry at first, that is understandable."

She thought that the one who would really be angry was the Duke and it was she who had to stand up to him.

But she knew that there was no point in saying so and she merely went on,

"All we need to concentrate on now is you getting away safely. It would be ghastly if you were stopped at the very last moment. I would be very terrified of what your father might do."

"There is nothing he can do once you are married," Henriet said, "But I quite understand, darling Caterina, you would have no wish to face the fury of not only one man but two."

She gave a little shudder as she added,

"I cannot think what the Duke will say. I wish you had kept my revolver in case he is cruel to you."

"If he is, I can always jump into the sea," Caterina said, "and it's no use thinking about it or worrying. Just enjoy yourself because you are with Fritz and don't worry about me."

"Of course I worry about you, but you are always so clever, Caterina, and I have a feeling that you will find a way to stop the Duke being as angry as he might be."

"I would not bet on that. At the same time what really matters, dearest, is that you are safe with Fritz and they cannot bring you back on any pretext."

"Fritz has thought of that and, of course, he will be changing his name."

Caterina looked at her in surprise.

"Will that be official?" she asked.

"Yes. Papa might well make it difficult for him if we went to some country where he might be traced."

Caterina gave a cry of horror as she had not thought of that possibility, but Henriet went on,

"In future we will be Monsieur and Madame Leon."

Caterina laughed.

"That at least is easy to remember."

"And the yacht," Henriet continued, "which had an Austrian name, is now *Rose Marie* and it will be French."

"That is sensible and will Fritz call you Marie?"

"He will call me a lot of things because he loves me, but Henriet dies tonight when she leaves the Palace. So I can be Rose Marie if I like or just Marie and no one will question for a single moment that I might be Princess Henriet."

"I can only congratulate you and Fritz for thinking of everything!"

"It is all Fritz really and, of course, he cannot be Fritz any longer."

"What has he chosen for himself?"

Henriet laughed.

"Victor! How could he be anything else, when he has won, thanks to you, the most difficult battle he has ever been engaged in? As he said, when he was a soldier, he would have been given a special medal!"

"I think you are both splendid," Caterina sighed.

"If I could give you a thousand medals, I would do so, darling wonderful Caterina, but please be in touch with us as soon as you can and don't forget that Madame Leon is now your friend and you address her as Rose Marie."

"I am sure I will not forget, but you are very wise. In fact I am only ashamed I did not think of it myself."

"You thought of everything essential," Henriet said, "and Fritz is determined to give you the most marvellous present we can possibly buy, which we will send to you in England. But you will have to be very careful not to let the Duke know who it is from."

It flashed through Caterina's mind that by that time the Duke might not be speaking to her or they might not even be together, but she thought it would only complicate matters if she said so.

"All I want to know," she said, "is if you change the place you are going to that you let me know where I can be in touch with you."

She sighed before she went on,

"After all, as I am giving up Austria, I would like to think that there is one other place in the world I can go to without people pointing their fingers at me."

"I will let you know everywhere we go and what we do," Henriet answered. "But you must remember our new names and, of course, the name of Fritz's yacht."

"I will remember everything," Caterina promised. "And all I am thinking of now is that you are going to be very happy and you are not to worry about anything, not even me."

"I will not only worry about you, but pray for you."

They talked for a little while longer and then Malca came into the room.

"All the guards," she said to Henriet, "are drinkin' your health and, if you asks me, they'll all be swayin' in another quarter-of-an-hour or so. They'll certainly not be capable of noticin' anythin' strange in the garden."

"What are they drinking," Caterina asked.

"Champagne, and enjoyin' every drop of it," Malca replied.

Henriet looked surprised.

"It does not sound like my father," she said, "to be so generous where wine is concerned."

Malca smiled.

"Perhaps I did misunderstand His Royal Highness's instructions when I said they were to have champagne in which to drink your health and I am almost sure he said it was a bottle to each man!"

Henriet gave a little cry.

"Oh, Malca! You made that up, you know you did! That does not sound in the least like Papa."

"I might have missed what His Royal Highness was sayin', because I was overwrought at your bein' married," Malca replied not very convincingly.

She looked round quickly before she added,

"Now come along. Let's get off while the coast's clear."

She helped Henriet into a light coat of a dark colour so that she would not be noticeable and then she gave her a handkerchief to put over her head.

As she went to pick up her handbag, Henriet put her arms round Caterina's neck and kissed her on both cheeks.

"Thank you, thank you, darling," she said, "there are no words in any language which express what I feel."

"All you have to do is be happy," Caterina said. "We have both used our brains and so has V-Victor."

She stumbled over the name and Henriet laughed.

"I know he will want to thank you a thousand times when he next sees you. In the meantime you know how grateful he is."

"All I wish is that you will be really happy and that is what I want to hear as soon as possible. I suppose you are being married at sea."

Henriet nodded.

"It is absolutely legal and, although it will be a very simple marriage, once I am Fritz's wife, I will not worry about anything again."

"No, of course not, I just wish I could be with you."

"We shall be together as soon as it's possible and that I hope will be sooner than we think."

She hugged Caterina again.

Then, as Malca opened the door, they slipped out and hurried along the corridor to the staircase they had used before, which led to the side door into the garden.

Caterina watched them go until they disappeared completely and then she went back into Henriet's bedroom.

From this moment she had to be Henriet and not herself and she hoped as she started to undress that she had remembered everything.

Earlier in the evening she had put together all the clothes in her bedroom, which she wanted Malca to take to the Battleship.

Malca had looked after her since she came to stay at the Palace and there was therefore no question of any other maid finding it strange that they had been packed up, but even so she locked her bedroom door.

'Is that everything?' she now asked herself as she climbed into Henriet's bed.

Although she had not expected to do so, she fell fast asleep and, when Malca came creeping into her room, having left Henriet in Fritz's care, she did not stir.

Malca stood looking at her for a moment and then blew out the candle by the bed which she had left alight.

She groped her way to the door to go to her own room and was muttering beneath her breath,

'Poor little child! I wonder what that hard-faced Englishman will do to her.'

*

Caterina woke early before Malca came to call her and her first thought was that it was a sunny day.

Her second was that she was being married to a man she had hardly spoken to and who had, she thought, ignored her as being of little significance.

'How could I have thought or even imagined for a moment when I came to stay here at the Palace,' she asked herself, 'that all this would happen to me?'

Anyway it had happened and now she had to face the music.

She could not pretend to herself that it was going to be easy, but she had thought it out very carefully.

She knew every word she spoke and every gesture she made had to be an imitation of Henriet.

She was still gazing out of the window at the bright sunshine and thinking over what lay ahead for her when Malca peeped in at the door.

"Oh, you are awake, Princess."

"What happened last night?" Caterina asked her. "I must have been asleep when you came back."

"Oh, it was wonderful. As I thought, there was no one about and we reached the hut safely."

"And he was waiting for you?"

"Yes, he was," Malca replied. "He'd taken all the luggage I'd given him durin' the day and there was just themselves, so to speak, to go to the yacht. It was waitin', he said, in a bay which was of no interest to anyone."

"And they are now happy?" Caterina said almost to herself.

"They are blissfully happy," Malca replied. "I've never seen two people so thrilled with each other."

She gave a chuckle before she continued,

"When 'my baby Henriet' says goodbye to me she says, 'don't forget, Malca, I cannot live without you and you must come to us as quickly as you can. But you must first look after Princess Caterina and tell her that thanks to her I am the happiest woman in the world'."

There was a sob in Malca's voice as she spoke the last words.

Then Caterina said,

"That is all I wanted to know."

"You've been marvellous, Princess, and I can only pray that things will come right for you."

"I will pray as well, because I don't think it's going to be at all easy."

There was no hurry and she had a comfortable bath, which Malca arranged for her.

Then she dressed slowly until she was ready to put on the beautiful wedding dress.

It was certainly a dream gown and the seamstresses must have worked for hours and hours to create a dress that any woman from any country would think glorious.

Malca arranged her hair under the tiara and the veil so that it would not show that it was not quite the same colour as Henriet's.

When she put on the wedding dress, it fitted her except for being a little looser than if it had been made for her, but Malca pinned it comfortably into place.

Then she produced the diamond and pearl necklace that the Duke had given Henriet.

"It makes this gown," she said, "and it's a pity 'my baby' isn't able to keep it."

Caterina smiled.

"I think Henriet would refuse to accept anything from him, even if it was not a family heirloom!"

"I expects," Malca said, "Monsieur Leon, as I now have to call him, will find one even prettier for his wife."

"I am sure he will," Caterina laughed.

Then her breakfast was brought up and taken in by Malca without the footman coming into the room.

Caterina drank the coffee and ate a little piece of *croissant* spread with honey, but she could not face the dish of eggs that had been provided for her.

"You'd better eat somethin'," Malca urged her, "we can't have you faintin' about the place."

"It is what I will have to pretend to do," Caterina replied. "I was thinking again it would be a good idea if you went to the Prince and told him that his daughter is extremely hysterical at the idea of leaving him and that he would be wise not to talk too much to her or in fact be at all affectionate. If he does, she might refuse to leave."

"I understand, Princess, I'll go and find His Royal Highness at once."

She left the room and Caterina locked the door behind her just in case anyone should burst in to give her their good wishes.

She kept thinking that by this time Henriet and the man she loved would be well out to sea.

In fact, they might already be married.

She sent up a prayer that they would be safe and able to hide in their new identity in a part of the world where no one would think of looking for them.

Perhaps such precautions were unnecessary, but at the same time she thought they were wise. No one ever quite knew, when things went wrong, how even the most staid man would behave.

Malca came back a short while later having seen the Prince in private.

"I tells His Royal Highness that his poor daughter is so unhappy at leavin' him she was threatenin' to refuse to be married even when he took her to the Cathedral. So, unless he wants a scene, he should keep her calm and not let her work herself up as she was doin' at the moment."

"What did he say?" Caterina asked.

"Oh, His Royal Highness agreed to everythin' I says to him. I said, 'just behave as if you were goin' out for a drive together. Don't mention the Duke. It'll be enough when she sees him in the Cathedral'."

"Did he listen to you attentively?"

"He listened to every word and I can say that His Royal Highness was really worried that there would be a scene in the Cathedral or in the carriage on the way there."

"That is just what I wanted," Caterina said, "and, of course, I will be wearing a veil."

When she put it on, she knew that Malca had been very clever. She had made the front part of the veil double the thickness that it was meant to be and it would be quite impossible for anyone seeing her as she walked up the aisle to suspect that it was not Henriet.

Caterina was well aware that the real difficulty would come when she had to leave the Cathedral, but she was sure that, if she kept her head down or maybe held a handkerchief to her eyes, she would get away with it.

"Now what you have to do, Malca, is to be waiting for me, if I get as far as the ship from the Cathedral, no one better than you could protect me from the man who will then be my husband."

"Leave that to me, Princess, but be very careful His Royal Highness does not find you are deceivin' him on the way to the Cathedral and the same goes for the Duke from the Cathedral to the Battleship."

"I have been thinking it out," Caterina said, "and I am determined that no one will have any idea that I am not Henriet until we are well out to sea. Then it will be just impossible for the Duke to turn round and take me back."

"I'll see he doesn't do that," Malca exclaimed.

Because she looked so fierce as she said it, Caterina laughed.

"I think between us both we ought to make quite certain that everything goes off without any trouble. Most of all we have to remember that every minute we remain on Austrian soil and then on the Battleship Henriet will by then be Madame Leon."

"God bless her," Malca murmured.

"She will be with her charming husband Victor," Caterina continued, "and whether the authorities like it or not, they will be married."

"God bless their souls," Malca repeated quietly and Caterina prayed for them as well.

CHAPTER FIVE

Caterina stared at herself in the mirror and decided that no one would recognise her, but she thought she must keep her head down and appear upset at leaving home.

She had asked Malca to go down again to the hall and she was to tell any of the staff, who were not going to the Cathedral and were waiting in the hall, not to try to say goodbye to her as it would upset her.

Malca came back smiling and said,

"It's all fixed. The stage is set for you to make sure that His Royal Highness has not the slightest idea that 'my baby' is not beside him."

"I will do my best," Caterina promised. "But pray hard and don't forget that I am relying on you to meet me when we reach the Battleship."

"You can trust me. God bless you, Princess, and I'll be prayin' all the time that nothin' will go wrong."

A footman appeared at the door to say that His Royal Highness was waiting in the hall.

When he had gone, Caterina deliberately waited five minutes, as she thought that it would make the Prince more anxious to reach the Cathedral quickly.

Finally she walked slowly down the wide staircase with Malca lifting her train behind her.

It was not long enough to need pages, but it was much easier for her to walk when it was lifted up.

Caterina kept her head well down and when she did appear, Prince Adolphus greeted her,

"Oh, here you are, dearest. I think we should hurry as I am told the Cathedral is already packed."

Caterina did not answer.

She went out through the door and climbed into the carriage. It was the one traditionally used for weddings and Royal occasions and was known as the 'Glass Coach' and it was easy through the thick clear glass to see two people seated inside it.

She thought, as she sat down, it would be difficult when they drove away from the Cathedral to prevent the crowd from seeing her closely.

Now it was easy to sit with bowed head behind the double veil, falling like curtains on either side of her face.

The Prince then climbed in on the other side and sat down beside her and the four white horses started off.

Although there had been very little time to notify the local people, there were already crowds on each side of the road and a number of small boys were waving flags.

The Prince raised his hand in the Royal fashion to the cheers as they passed.

Caterina did not move or speak.

She was aware that there was a bouquet laid ready for her on the seat in front of her and she thought that the orchids in it were very beautiful.

She tried not to think of anything except what was happening immediately and not to anticipate the dangers as they drove to the Battleship.

The crowds grew bigger and bigger as they neared the Cathedral.

The Square in front of it was absolutely packed with people.

Caterina could not help wondering if there were any Russians amongst them and what were they thinking of this union between Istria and Great Britain.

The Glass Coach drew up at the Cathedral below the long line of steps leading up to the West door.

A red carpet had been laid over them and already there were children on each side holding flowers.

Caterina knew that they would throw them in front of her when she came out with her bridegroom.

She waited before alighting from the Glass Coach until the Prince was beside her to take his arm.

She held onto him as if she was nervous and scared – which actually she was.

The footman from the Glass Coach then arranged her train so that it spread out behind her as she walked.

"There is no hurry," the Prince murmured. "Just take your time up those steps. I don't want you to stumble or to feel breathless."

He had not spoken to her in the Glass Coach and she reckoned that Malca had done her job well.

Now was the final test of whether she would be able to keep up the deception and marry the Duke to save Henriet.

As they entered the West door, the organ began to play and, peeping through her veil, Caterina saw that the Cathedral really was packed 'from floor to ceiling'.

Most of the congregation she knew must be from the City, as it would have been impossible at such short notice for any Royals to travel such a long distance from their own countries.

Very slowly the Prince drew Caterina up the aisle and she was aware that every head in every pew was turned in her direction.

As she passed the choir, she saw waiting at the altar rails the tall figure of the Duke.

He was wearing a uniform on which there were a number of decorations with the blue Order of the Garter across his chest.

In fact Caterina thought with a little smile that he was dressed up for the occasion as much as she was.

She handed her bouquet to an attendant, as well as her gloves, which she had taken it off just before she left the Glass Coach.

Malca had warned her to keep her gloves on until the very last moment, as her hands were rather larger than Henriet's and, if the Prince touched her, he might realise it.

The Archbishop of Istria, wearing embroidered and bejewelled vestments, started the Marriage Service in a deep authoritative voice.

Caterina realised with relief that it must have been on the Prince's orders that it was as short as possible and the choir sang beautifully and she was sorry that she would be unable to congratulate them.

Then came the moment when the ring she had tried on before was blessed.

Next the Duke placed it on her finger.

He said his vows in a firm calm voice and Caterina deliberately made her responses just a little louder than a whisper.

After their hands were ceremonially joined together by the Archbishop, they knelt to receive the Blessing.

It was now that Caterina began to pray frantically that she would not make a mistake and all would go well.

She not only asked God for His help but also her mother.

Then, as the choir sang the beginning of an anthem, they processed slowly into the Vestry.

This was a seriously dangerous moment.

Caterina knew that she had to sign her name and to do so she was expected to lift her veil.

Quickly she drew from the belt round her waist a soft white handkerchief that Malca had placed there.

When one of the attendant Priests carefully raised the veil from her face, she put her handkerchief up to her eyes as if she was crying.

Fortunately there was not much light in the Vestry and, when she wrote Henriet's name speedily, she pulled down her long veil so that it covered one side of her face and her handkerchief concealed the other side.

Then the trumpets blared and the organ began to play the Royal March that had been used at weddings for over two hundred years.

The Duke offered Caterina his arm and they started to walk down the aisle towards the West door and he was wise enough not to go too fast.

Someone had pulled her train into position behind her and she made no effort to take the bouquet which was being handed back to her.

Instead she lifted her handkerchief to her eyes.

With her head lowered, her veil covering her left cheek and her handkerchief the other, it was impossible for anyone to recognise her.

When they reached the West door, Caterina saw, as she had expected, a crowd of children holding flowers and petals to throw in front of her.

Because she did not want to disappoint them, she smiled at those who were on her left hand side, but she was very careful not to let the Duke, even if he had looked, see her face.

When they arrived at the Glass Coach, a footman helped her into the near seat.

The Duke went round to the other side and, amid cheers from the crowd in the Square, climbed in beside her.

The horses moved off, but they were unable to go at all quickly owing to the fact that small boys were running beside the coach, some throwing flowers.

They fell at the feet of the bride and bridegroom and the pile gradually increased.

Then the horses turned off the main road that led to the Palace and trotted instead towards the river.

There were not so many children or flowers to be seen here and Caterina felt that she could relax a little, but kept her handkerchief up to her eyes.

The Duke had not said one word to her since they had left the Cathedral and, owing to the loud cheers of the crowd, it would have been difficult to hear him anyway.

It was fortunately only a very short distance to the Quay where the Battleship from England was waiting and at a quick glance Caterina realised that it was even more impressive than she had expected it to be.

As it was decorated with Union Jacks, it certainly looked very grand and overpowering.

Then, as they started to walk up the gangway to the ship, the Duke spoke for the first time,

"I must present you to the Captain," he said, "and to the other Officers.

"I feel rather faint," Caterina murmured.

As she spoke, she put her two hands over her face and to her considerable surprise the Duke acted quickly without questioning her.

He picked her up in his arms and carried her up the gangway.

They then passed the Battleship Officers standing to attention as they were piped aboard.

The Duke carried her across the deck and down the companionway and she was conscious that he was strong and tall.

She realised that he did not find her at all heavy, although her train made going down the steps somewhat difficult.

Then, as he paused to lift it, Malca, from where she had been waiting, came running towards them.

"Is Her Royal Highness all right?" she asked.

"She said she felt a little faint," the Duke replied, "so I thought that she should lie down."

"Yes, that is very wise of Your Grace," Malca said. "Please bring her into the cabin and I will take care of her."

The Duke walked down the passage and Caterina, with her hands over her face, did not open her eyes.

Then she felt herself being put down gently onto a bed and heard Malca saying,

"Now leave her in my hands, Your Grace. I'll look after her and it be best after all the nervous strain of the weddin' that she be not disturbed."

"Just ask my valet for anything you require," the Duke said.

Then Caterina heard the door close and lowered her hands.

"Did everything go off well?" Malca asked her in a whisper.

"Everything," Caterina replied. "I don't think there was one person present who had the least suspicion that I was not who they expected."

Malca turned the key in the door and suggested,

"You should undress and go to bed, Princess. You must, as you know, keep out of sight till we are well out to sea."

Caterina had noticed when she came aboard that the engines were already turning over.

Now she was aware that there were loud cheers from the quayside outside and the ship began to move.

She expected that the Duke was up on deck waving to the crowd and somewhere in the distance she could hear a band playing.

Caterina felt it was sad that the people were cheated of the big farewell they had intended to give their Princess when she married and she was sure that the children with flowers and women with presents would be disappointed.

The only thing, however, that really mattered was that Henriet was now safe for ever.

Caterina could only hope that the Duke would not be vindictive enough to try to hurt her and her husband once he discovered the truth.

Malca quickly took off Caterina's veil, her tiara and then the pearl necklace. Next she undid the wedding dress and it fell to the ground.

"It's so pretty," Caterina sighed, "that it's so sad it will never be worn again."

"Don't be sure of that," Malca chipped in. "If you have a daughter she'd be thrilled to wear it. As it's the prettiest gown I've ever seen, it'll doubtless end up in a museum."

Caterina laughed and then instinctively she put her finger to her lips.

"You don't think anyone could be listening to us?" she asked in a whisper."

I doubt it," Malca replied. "The walls of this ship be strong and thick, but it's best to whisper till we're well out to sea."

"I must remember that."

She climbed into bed and Malca pulled the curtains over the portholes.

Caterina had to admit it was a comfortable cabin and, almost as if she had asked her the question, Malca explained,

"This be the Captain's cabin and I don't suppose he really likes givin' it up to you."

"I feel sure he begrudges it," Caterina agreed.

Then in a more anxious voice she asked,

"Where is the Duke sleeping?"

"Next door. This is the only good cabin in the ship. The others are small and not nearly so comfortable."

Caterina drew in her breath.

She knew without Malca saying any more that it was expected that the Duke and she would be sharing the Captain's bed.

Other cabins, which were just for the Officers were frugal. It was a warship and those on it did not expect to enjoy comforts as if they were on a holiday steamer.

"I suggested," Malca said, still speaking in a low voice, "that you would like some flowers. But I were told this was a ship of war and they did not have such frivolous items as flowers on board."

"I suppose my bouquet was left behind," Caterina said. "It was so lovely I am sorry to part with it."

"You cannot have your cake and eat it, Princess. What we have to be right thankful for is that the ceremony went off all right. I was holdin' my breath all the time you was away just in case some nosy-parker jumped to his feet and said, 'this ain't the bride we was promised'!"

Caterina laughed.

"I was afraid of that too, except that I had so many veils to cope with that I could hardly see through them!"

"Veils or no veils there're a lot of people who are goin' to feel they have been 'had' when it becomes known their Princess is not, as they thought, now a real English Duchess, but just an ordinary woman, whose heart is of more value than any title."

"That is true enough. What I suggest you do now is find us both a nice cup of coffee, Malca."

To her surprise Malca shook her head.

"You are not allowed that," she said, "because I'm goin' to tell His Grace that you're asleep and I'll not have you disturbed."

"Of course, I am crazy. I forgot the Duke must not see me until we are well out to sea and if possible not for another two days."

"You will not die of starvation," Melca said with a smile. "I've brought aboard with me quite enough food which you can eat when no one is watchin' and a bottle of His Royal Highness's best champagne. I'm goin' to give you a glass of it now."

"That, of course, is very appropriate for a wedding breakfast," Caterina said sarcastically. "It was clever of you, Malca, to think of it."

She drank the champagne, although Malca refused a glass. She claimed it was a drink she did not particularly care for.

"Now I'm goin' to lock you in," she said, "to be sure no one wakes you up and I'm goin' up on deck to find out what's planned."

Caterina was aware that the Battleship had been increasing speed ever since they had left Port and now she was certain that they were out to sea and going faster still.

Malca had provided her with some biscuits to eat while she drank the champagne and, as she was no longer hungry or for the moment frightened, she then lay down thankfully on what was an extremely comfortable mattress.

It was, of course, traditional for the Captain of a ship to have a bed and, in all other ships she had visited, it had been a four-poster.

*

Malca was away for a long time and, when she returned, she was full of information.

"His Grace's havin' a delicious luncheon," she said. "In fact, the chef from the Palace brought it aboard on His Royal Highness's orders."

"While I have had nothing but biscuits," Caterina pretended to complain.

Malca laughed.

"No, you're bein' spoilt, and I've been very clever about it. I struck up a friendship with His Grace's valet when he came to the Palace. He's promised to bring me some of the dishes I really likes. We'll therefore be eatin' Palace food for the beginnin' of our voyage."

"Oh, you are clever, Malca!" Caterina exclaimed.

The chef at the Palace had been outstanding and, anxious though she had been about Henriet, she had to admit that she had enjoyed every meal.

Now it was a relief to think she would have good food to eat even though she was supposed to be an invalid.

When Malca brought her luncheon, she enjoyed it all the more being so relieved that the ordeal was over and everything had gone better than she had dared to hope.

She only wished they would be sailing as quickly as possible to a secret destination, where if things had gone wrong and the Prince had ordered for her to be brought back, she then hoped it would be impossible to find her.

'We have been really extremely clever,' Caterina thought. 'At the same time I, myself, am not yet out of the woods.'

Even to think of the Duke made her shiver.

Yet she kept telling herself that, however angry he might be, there would be nothing he could do about it once they were well on their way to England and by that time Henriet and Fritz would have disappeared completely.

When her luncheon was over, Malca unpacked the books Caterina had put in with her dresses. These were books she wanted to read, but had not had the time and she was a very quick reader.

She asked Malca to find out if there were any other books on board.

"I think you be askin' too much," Malca replied. "But I'll have a look round and find anythin' I can."

She was away for some time and then she returned with three English books, which she said she had obtained from His Grace's valet.

"His Grace?" Caterina exclaimed in surprise.

"Well, apparently His Grace always travels with a number of books. Whatever you say, it'll be good for you to read in English, seein' as how that's what you'll have to talk in the future, whether you like it or not."

"That is certainly true, Malca. It will be useful for me to polish up my English, even though I flatter myself it is quite good."

When she examined them, she found that they were different from what she had expected the Duke to read.

One was a historical biography which she knew she would enjoy and another was a novel by one of the best known English authors and the third, to her surprise, was a history of Austria written in English.

She had somehow not thought that the Duke would do his homework before coming to Istria, but he had quite obviously wished to know more about the background of the Princess he was marrying and she had to give him top marks for that.

He had seemed so indifferent when he was at the Palace that she had somehow thought that he would only be interested in his own country and that he would make no effort to acquaint himself with the country of Austria even if he was marrying someone to whom it meant everything.

"I will read this one to start with," Caterina said. "Then you will have to find out what more the Duke has with him."

"I understands," Malca said, "there's also a place where they keep implements for games. There were books there and magazines for the men when they have time and packs of cards. The valet tells me they enjoys bridge."

"Well, find out everything you can. I don't want to make silly mistakes when I do appear and, as you well know, we don't know much about the English."

"Except that they give themselves airs because they thinks they are important. The valet is a nice man, but he talks to me as if I were a child of six with no brains!"

Caterina grinned.

"Papa says all the English are like that, puffed up with their own importance. In a way one can understand it, considering that Queen Victoria now rules three-quarters of the world."

"Well, that's her business," Malca asserted. "All I can tell you is that I'm quite content to be 'Miss Nobody' as long as I can be with those I love and who love me."

"That's true enough, Malca, and you know Henriet will be counting the days until you join her."

"God bless her sweet little heart. I knows she's happy now that she be married and no one can take her off to England no matter how much they try."

She paused before she added,

"If there's one place I don't want to go, then it's England!"

"You must not say that to me, because if ever I am accepted there, the first person I will ask to stay is Henriet and, of course, you must come with her too."

"Oh, if I was with you that would be different, Princess, but I cannot help thinkin' you will find it hard to make whatever house His Grace lives in a place of laughter and fun as things used to be at the Palace."

When she was alone, Caterina began thinking over what Malca had just said and she thought what she really longed for and needed was laughter and amusement.

Austrians always loved music and her mother had taught her to play the piano as well as she played herself and when she was alive she often danced with her husband in the evening just because it made her happy.

'I just cannot imagine the English doing that,' she thought, 'and certainly *not* the Duke.'

She was aware that the ship was now moving at full speed instead of pulling into a quiet bay for the night as a private yacht would have done.

'The Duke is obviously in a hurry to return home,' she thought. 'At this rate it will not take us very long.'

She read until she fell asleep.

*

The next morning she unlocked the cabin door and Malca came in.

"The Duke," she said "is askin' if you feel well enough to join him on deck. The sun is shinin' and the sea is calm."

Caterina gave a little shudder.

"I suppose I must eventually get it over with. How far have we gone now, Malca?"

"Further than I expected and I will ask where we will be callin'. I should think it will not be long now before we reach Brindisi."

Caterina did not say anything more. At the same time she realised that Malca was longing, although she did not say so, to disembark and joint Henriet as planned.

It was at Brindisi she would receive the information as to where they were in Fritz's yacht.

She was only afraid, as the Duke was obviously in such a hurry to return home, that they might not put into a Port at all and then Malca would be very worried as to how she could join Henriet.

Also Caterina found it rather boring to be shut up all day in the cabin when the sun was shining outside and she longed to be on deck to watch the waves breaking over the bow.

She loved the sea and, because Theiss was not near the sea as Istria was, she had always enjoyed her visits to Henriet more than anywhere else she went.

However, she felt that she must postpone facing the Duke until they had gone too far to turn back and she then told Malca to make her excuses.

*

It was late in the afternoon when Malca came into her cabin to say,

"His Grace says he'll be very pleased if you feel well enough to join him at dinner tonight. I've told him you

101

were sleepin' most of the time and were now calmer than you were when you left home. But I thought it a mistake for you to do too much too soon."

Caterina giggled.

"You make it sound as if I am completely decrepit. In fact I am beginning to feel like it shut up in here."

"Well, if you asks me, it's safe from one point of view for you to dine with His Grace. After all you have to meet him sooner or later."

"I know that," Caterina replied, "and perhaps it will be easier if I get it over with in the evening. If he is very disagreeable, I can lock myself in my cabin for another twenty-four hours."

Malca waited and then she asked,

"What shall I tell His Grace, Princess?"

"What time is dinner?" Caterina asked.

"I suppose about eight o'clock."

"Very well. Tell His Grace I will join him at seven o'clock and, if it is warm enough, I would like to stroll on deck before we sit down to dinner."

Malca made no comment and left the cabin.

When she had gone, Caterina wondered if she had made a mistake.

Then she thought, however much they raged at each other, they would be obliged to stop and go to bed before very long.

At the same time she was frightened and could not pretend otherwise.

She had a bath and then Malca took out of the small wardrobe in the cabin one of her very prettiest and most attractive evening gowns.

She had bought it just before going to Istria and she had been assured that it was a Paris model.

Her father had reluctantly paid a high price for it, but she felt it was worth every schilling he had paid.

Malca arranged her hair and when she looked in the mirror Caterina hesitated.

"Shall I wear the diamond necklace His Grace gave Henriet?" she asked.

"I thinks that would be addin' insult to injury. Just go as your nice friendly self. After all, if you upsets him more than you are bound to do anyway, you are still his wife and you may have to put up with him for a long time."

"You are so right, Malca. It's only because I am nervous that I am likely to do silly things."

"We all do sooner or later, but you've been so sensible, so kind and such a great friend to 'my baby' that I can only think of you as the nicest woman I've ever met."

"Thank you, Malca. But at the moment I don't feel like a woman, more like a child who has been very naughty at school and is wondering what punishment she is going to receive."

There was a tremor in her voice which told Malca more than words what she was feeling.

"Now you listen to me, Princess, you're one of the prettiest women His Grace is ever likely to meet. If you asks me, he hasn't got such a bad bargain. Henriet, as you and I well know, gets hysterical and very difficult if she doesn't have her own way."

Caterina smiled because this was so true.

"But you are different," Malca went on. "You have always been wise, you have always been the leader, the one your friends have turned to when they be in trouble. So don't think of yourself as being a burden to anyone. Remember it's His Grace who's in trouble now!"

"You mean because he is going back to England with the wrong wife?"

"Exactly. It's not goin' to be easy for him and, if he asks for your help, how can you refuse him?"

Caterina laughed.

"Oh, Malca, you are wonderful! You always say the right thing at the right moment. Of course I must think of him and stop worrying about myself."

She bent and kissed Malca and continued,

"Henriet is very lucky to have you always with her. Although I will hate to lose you, I know her need is greater than mine and you must go to her just as soon as we reach Brindisi?"

"I was told," Malca said, "that we ought to get there by tomorrow night."

"As I will need all my wits about me, then the sooner I step into the lions' den, the better."

"There's only one lion in it," Malca replied, "and if you ask me, I'm rather sorry for him!"

Caterina laughed and then she walked out of her cabin and along the passage to what she had been told was the Captain's sitting room and like his bedroom it had been given over to the visitors.

The Duke was sitting in a comfortable chair reading a newspaper and, when Caterina came in through the door, he looked up.

Then, as he rose to his feet, he exclaimed,

"Princess Caterina! I had no idea that you were on board."

Caterina walked towards him.

"I am on board," she said in a small nervous voice, "because – I have taken Henriet's place, while – she has gone and married – someone else."

The Duke stared at her.

"What are you saying? I don't understand."

Whether it was due to the movement of the ship or because she felt nervous, Caterina sat down.

"I am afraid that you will be very angry," she said slowly. "But Henriet is in love with someone else and so that she – could marry him, I then – took her place in the Cathedral."

The Duke sat down next to her and then he said,

"Are you telling me that I am married to *you?*"

Caterina nodded her head.

"Is Prince Adolphus aware of this?" he enquired.

"No, of course not! Henriet is deeply in love with a man who is not Royal. She knew when she was told that she was to marry you that there was no possible escape, except, as she intended to do, by killing herself."

"Rather than marry me?" the Duke asked.

"Rather than marry anyone except for the man she loves. He loves her just as deeply and the only way I could save her life – was to take her place. No one – has the slightest idea that I have done so except Malca who, as you know, was Henriet's Nanny."

"I must be very stupid," the Duke said, "but I just cannot understand how this could have happened under the Prince's nose and he was not aware of it."

"Henriet eloped the night before the wedding and is now married to the man she loves and with whom she will be very happy."

"What I cannot understand is why she did not tell her father that she had no wish to marry me."

"Of course she told her father when she was first informed that it had been arranged for you to come to Istria, but because the marriage was the Emperor's wish, Uncle Adolphus, as I call him, would not listen."

She paused to draw in her breath and then went on,

"Henriet, rather than be married to any man but the man she loves, was determined to kill herself. She has always been like a sister to me and I could not bear to let her do that."

"So you took her place," the Duke said slowly as if he was thinking it out. "And no one had any suspicion that you were not who you pretended to be."

Because he was not shouting at her and seemed not as furiously angry as she expected, Caterina answered quite calmly,

"Henriet, as probably you don't know – is a very highly strung and emotional girl. Her father was afraid she would make a scene at the wedding or, as she told him, that she would kill herself rather than be married to a man she did not love."

"You really think she meant it?" the Duke asked.

"She certainly meant it. As I have told you, she is a very sensitive person and she is wildly madly in love with a man who loves her."

She thought the Duke was beginning to understand and went on,

"I thought that there was absolutely no chance of their ever being together. He is an Officer in the Prince's Special Guard and a gentleman, but not in the least Royal."

"And the Emperor wanted a Royal marriage and a strong tie with Great Britain," the Duke said, "because it would strengthen the position of Austria in relation to the Russians."

The Duke spoke as if he was still thinking it out quietly to himself.

"I hoped you would understand. It was impossible to go against the Emperor's wishes as well as her father's, so what could Henriet do but run away and hope that they will never find her and her husband?"

"Do you think the Prince will try to find them?" the Duke asked.

"I think that depends entirely on you. If you make a terrible row about it, they might try to bring Henriet back and arrest or even execute her husband."

"What is the alternative?" the Duke enquired.

There was silence for a moment and then Caterina responded,

"That you accept me without making a fuss."

"Why should I do that?"

"Because, although my father is not of the same stature as Prince Adolphus, he is Royal and also a distant cousin of the Emperor and the Kingdom of Theiss is part of Austrian history in the same way that Istria is, only they are more important than we are."

Without saying anything the Duke rose and walked to the porthole.

He stood looking out at the waves and Caterina waited.

'At least,' she mused, 'he is not raging at me. But he may still throw me off at the next Port of call.'

The minutes seemed to tick by and then the Duke said without turning round,

"I am bewildered. Quite frankly I cannot think how all this could have happened without my having even the slightest suspicion of it."

"We were very careful and worked out every detail. Henriet was married before we were and, even if you had exposed me as an imposter, you would still not have been able to marry her."

The Duke turned from the porthole and came back to sit down again.

"What do you think His Royal Highness is going to say when he learns what has happened?" he asked.

"He will be furious, really furious, but he cannot do anything unless you force him to do so."

She looked questioningly at the Duke, but he did not speak.

"I have thought it over every night since I arrived at the Palace. I knew that you were coming from England to marry someone you had never met, someone who, when you did arrive, you treated in such an offhand manner that it would have upset and distressed any woman."

"Was I rude?" the Duke asked.

"Yes, very, if you want the truth," Caterina replied. "You seemed deliberately to ignore Henriet and, although she was frightened and tried to avoid you, I thought that you were unnecessarily indifferent and cold."

To her astonishment the Duke laughed.

"I suppose I did behave badly," he said. "Because if she was upset, so was I."

Caterina's eyes opened wide.

"*You*? You did not want to marry Henriet?"

"Of course I did not," he replied. "I was sent for by the Queen and told what the Emperor required. As the Queen could think of no one else at that particular moment, I was told quite firmly, in fact ordered, that I was to go to Austria and marry Princess Henriet of Istria at once."

He paused before he continued,

"There was no question of my arguing about it. It was an order and, as it came from Her Majesty the Queen, I could only obey it or else I imagine be dismissed from Court if not worse."

"I never thought of that happening. I now see your difficulties as well as ours."

"I saw my own difficulties only too clearly," the Duke said. "I am now twenty-seven and have managed to avoid matrimony. I have been pursued, although perhaps it sounds conceited to say so, ever since I left school, simply because I am a Duke. And I always hoped that I would find someone who would love me for myself and not just for my title."

He gave a deep sigh and went on,

"Now you can see what has happened to me. I am married to someone I have hardly even spoken to and who has made it crystal clear that she thinks I am ill-mannered and arrogant."

Just as he had laughed, Caterina did the same.

"You are not quite as bad as that, but then you were rather frightening. In fact I have been terrified ever since I went to the Cathedral and became your wife and am no less scared now."

"I suppose all that commotion about your fainting and having to rest without seeing me was part of the plan?"

"Actually it was very boring as I longed to come up on deck and see the ship and I love being at sea," Caterina answered. "But I was grateful for the loan of your books, although they surprised me."

"What books?"

"Malca obtained them from your valet. I did not expect that you would have troubled to read up the history of Austria."

"Is that what he gave you? I can assure you I have many more interesting books than those."

"I have read two of them, as I have been polishing up my English."

"Your English is perfect," he said. "That is one consolation I found when I arrived at the Palace. Prince Adolphus speaks very good English, whilst the Princess's English is faultless, as is yours."

"We studied together and I enjoyed learning the languages of many countries in Europe," Caterina told him. "Without being conceited, I can tell you that I learnt more than Henriet did."

"So you were perhaps keen to go to England?"

"I would very much like to go to England, but I was not anxious to do so as your wife. In fact I too had hoped I would fall in love with someone who loved me and we would be as happy as my father and mother were. I can assure you that Henriet is blissfully happy."

She paused before she added,

"She has married a man who loves her because she is herself and not because she is a Royal Princess. He is fortunately very rich and could have married any number of other women."

"Where are they at this moment?" the Duke asked.

Caterina made a gesture with her hands.

"I am not sure and in any case neither you nor her father are likely to find them. They have the whole world to hide in and I am praying that you will leave them alone and forget all about them."

"That is all very well, but I can hardly forget about you. What do you think the Prince will say when he learns what has happened?"

Before Caterina could reply, he gave a sigh.

"I am naturally wondering also what they will say in England. Of course they will laugh at me for being so foolish as to marry the wrong bride."

"I am sorry for you, but perhaps we can think of a way to make it appear less ridiculous."

Then she gave a little cry.

"I said 'we', but I now am quite prepared for you to throw me overboard or deposit me on some uninhabited island and leave me to perish!"

She spoke quite seriously and, although she did not expect it, the Duke laughed.

"I think if I did either, I should expect to have a worse reputation than I have already."

"Have you a bad one?" Caterina asked.

"It depends on what you call bad. I have enjoyed myself as a single man and I have unfortunately, as I think now, dabbled in politics and been concerned, as the Queen has, with the aggression of the Russians."

He made a gesture with his hands and finished,

"It has ended in finding myself in this unexpected mess."

"I am afraid it is a mess, but I am sure we can find some way by which you can justify yourself so that no one is angry with you."

"Angry is hardly the right word. They will laugh at me and I doubt if I will ever be able to put my head inside Windsor Castle again."

"Is that worrying you?" Caterina questioned.

"Not really. It's just that I have tried to follow my traditions and, having fought for my country, I thought I should go on fighting for the peace of Europe."

Caterina was rather impressed by this statement and she could understand the difficulty he was now in.

"What are you thinking?" the Duke asked sharply, almost as if he was reading her thoughts.

"I was just thinking that, as I seem to have forced you into this trouble, I must try to get you out of it. I was able to solve Henriet's problem for her and perhaps, even though I could not make you any promises, I could in some magical way solve yours."

"It will certainly have to be magical, but I suppose I should be grateful to you for not sending me away from Istria empty-handed."

He spoke with a note of sarcasm in his voice and Caterina laughed.

"Perhaps we have been unkind to you and I had to make sure that Henriet escaped completely. I was terrified that her father would send his entire fleet and, perhaps your Battleship as well, to bring them back."

Her voice sank to a whisper as she finished,

"If he had, her husband would undoubtedly have been arrested and somehow disposed of."

"You really think that would have happened?"

Caterina nodded.

"Prince Adolphus can be hugely strict and is very proud where his family is concerned. He would have been furious if he had had to send you away without fulfilling the Emperor's orders."

"What do you think he will do now?"

Again Caterina made a gesture of helplessness.

"He will be very very angry and I am only hoping that you will not send me back."

The Duke looked at her.

"Perhaps that is what I ought to do."

"Oh, please spare me that," Caterina begged him. "Unless, of course, you just let me creep away as Henriet did. Only I sadly would have to go alone."

"And I unfortunately have a wife whom I did not want in the first place and who turns out to be someone quite different from the one the Emperor and the Prince of Istria had agreed upon!"

"I am so very sorry to have upset you!"

She spoke sincerely.

Then again the Duke laughed.

"I don't believe this is happening," he said. "It's just like a very bad dream or a comedy in the theatre and one has no idea of how it will end."

"I see what you mean," Caterina remarked. "Only I fear it may not be a comedy."

Again the Duke laughed.

CHAPTER SIX

Caterina stared at the Duke.

"Are you really finding this funny?" she asked.

"Not really. I feel sorry for you and I am sorry for myself. But now we are in this mess we have to put our heads together and find out how we can get out of it."

Caterina sighed.

"I have been thinking of how to 'get out' of messes ever since I arrived at the Palace. It was not an easy task to save Henriet from herself or indeed to pretend to be her at the wedding."

"You acted magnificently," the Duke said. "I was completely deceived. I thought that you were the difficult hysterical woman I expected you to be."

The way he spoke made it sound funny and then Caterina replied,

"We must be serious about this. I need to write to my father for one thing and explain what has happened and I am sure that he will *not* think it amusing."

"I am certain he will not," the Duke agreed. "You said that you are not sure where the two people are who have created this amazing muddle for us."

"The only person who will know for sure will be my lady's maid. As Henriet cannot live without her, Malca will leave us at Brindisi and disappear."

The Duke put his hands up to his forehead.

"If any more of these theatrical dramas happen, I will simply not believe them!"

"There is nothing theatrical about this. Malca, who has been looking after me on the Battleship, is in reality Henriet's Nanny whom she adores."

"The main trouble, as far as I can see, is where do I come in? I was sent for at a moment's notice to marry a Princess, who has married someone else and instead I have a Princess who has appeared to accept me, but at the same time admits to disliking me."

"I did not say 'dislike'," Caterina said. "But you were very frightening and poor Henriet was terrified of you."

"Perhaps you can understand that I had no wish to come to Istria and certainly no wish at all to marry some tiresome young girl just because she was a Princess and her father wanted support from Queen Victoria."

"You certainly made that very clear in the way you looked and the very little you said," Caterina replied.

Then she added quickly,

"I am not criticising. I told myself the only way I could stop you being furious with me was to be very soft, quiet and agreeable."

"So you had everything planned out."

"It was very frightening to do what I did," Caterina said in a small voice.

"Of course it was and I must say that you did it extremely well."

"That is high praise, but as far as I can see, there are very many stumbling-blocks ahead for you and the best thing you can do is to drop me overboard."

"I think that would be a wicked waste of a very pretty young woman, who is quite different from how I expected her to be."

"You have said that already and I must have made a very bad impression on you when we met. Of course, you were prejudiced anyway before you arrived."

"Very prejudiced indeed. In fact I became angrier and angrier every mile of the way."

"Now you can easily understand why you appeared so terrifying to us girls."

"Well, let's forget that for the moment," the Duke suggested, "and think of the future. What on earth am I going to say when I arrive in London or more specifically at Windsor Castle?"

Caterina gave a sudden cry.

The Duke stared at her in astonishment.

"I have thought of it. I have thought of an answer. It has come to me just as if Heaven itself worked it out for me."

"Tell me what this miraculous idea is – "

"Now let me think it out slowly and carefully. You arrived in Istria furious because you had been ordered by Her Majesty Queen Victoria that you were to marry an unknown Princess, simply because the Emperor of Austria had thought a closer connection with Britain would be a better safeguard against the Russians.

"That is right, but I don't think that the Emperor believed that the Russians would actually invade Austria. But they might easily infiltrate into outlying Provinces and cause trouble – especially those that are close to the sea."

Caterina nodded.

"Yes, I have heard the one thing they want more than anything else is to gain access to the Mediterranean."

"Well, go on."

"When you arrived in Istria," Caterina said, "you were told secretly by me that Henriet was married already to the man she loved."

The Duke stared at her.

"She was already married," he repeated. "Yes, I can see the significance of that. In fact I had made my journey for nothing."

"I also told you, and this is most important, that she was frightened that the man she loved, now her husband, might be arrested or even disposed of, because he was a commoner. You therefore must pretend to marry her and she had already made me promise to take her place."

The Duke thought for a moment and then he said,

"Yes, that seems reasonable."

"The point is, if you had exposed Henriet as you might have done, you would have been causing the death or at least life imprisonment of her husband and she would undoubtedly have killed herself rather than live without him."

"So," the Duke stated, "I accepted your suggestion and married you, masquerading as her."

"Exactly. You were apparently carrying out the wishes of the Emperor and of the Prince of Istria, while the latter was not aware of what his daughter had done."

The Duke thought for a moment.

"That is very clever of you," he said. "In fact I am certain that the Queen would accept it as the only possible thing I could do in the circumstances."

"That is what I thought. You could hardly marry a girl who was already married and to go back empty-handed would have delighted the Russians, who might easily have then stirred up an enormous amount of trouble in Istria."

"And are you going to tell this same story to your father?" the Duke asked her.

"I think if we are sensible that you should ask the advice of Her Majesty the Queen. It would undoubtedly be a shock to her and perhaps it would be better to keep silent for a short time."

"The same, I think, would apply to your father."

"Papa is a very clever man, at the same time a very practical one. I am quite certain that he will understand my horrible predicament that Henriet would undoubtedly kill herself rather than marry you. I am absolutely certain that my dear mother, if she was alive, would say that I had done the right thing."

"I think you are a very unusual young woman! We must think this over very carefully and try to hurt as few people as possible if they have to know the truth."

"I cannot help feeling that the longer we take the better. At present everyone is excited by the wedding and will talk of nothing else. In a month or more there will be another sensation or excitement to discuss and the wedding will slide into the background."

"You have an answer to everything," the Duke said, "although you are kind enough to ask my opinion, I cannot think of any idea that is better than yours."

"Then you agree? That is wonderful. Thank you! Thank you and I think as we don't want people to talk, I must remain as Princess Henriet until we reach England."

"Of course," the Duke agreed, "that is very wise and sensible. The only person you will have to tell what we are doing is Henriet herself."

"Malca will do so when she finds out where she is and joins them, as she will as soon as we reach Brindisi."

"Can you manage without a lady's maid until we reach England?"

"I am sure that your valet will fasten me up at the back and, as there is only you and I of any consequence on this exciting ship, I will not have to worry too much about my appearance."

The Duke looked at her.

"Shall I tell you that you are extremely beautiful?" he asked. "In fact, one of the most beautiful women I have ever seen."

"Do you really mean that? Or are you just being polite?"

"I hope I am being both. But it's true."

"I am supposed to be just like my mother, who was considered the most beautiful woman in Austria," Caterina added. "But she was much lovelier than I am."

"I am not prepared to argue about that," the Duke said. "Only to say how I see you and to be honest I am very impressed."

Caterina laughed.

"I did not expect you to say that the first moment we met. In point of fact I was expecting you to rage and shout at me, perhaps even hit me."

"I intend to do none of those things, but I think it would be interesting to get to know each other. You are certainly very different from what I anticipated."

"It will be fun getting to know each other and when we reach England and you have to reveal the truth of who I am, perhaps, if nothing else, we will part good friends."

"So you are seriously considering leaving me?" the Duke said. "Do you realise that, if you do, I will be unable to marry anyone else and my family who, for the last five years, have been begging me on their knees to marry, will be in floods of tears."

Caterina laughed.

"I have heard that story before. All families want the head of it to produce an heir immediately. I have always been sorry for the man who is forced up the aisle with some girl who has tricked him or else he marries the woman he really wants in the face of opposition from his relations."

"I see you have been reading English literature," the Duke said. "May I congratulate you again on your English, which is perfect."

"Henriet and I insisted on being taught most of the languages of Europe. I was more eager than she was, but you must admit our English is good."

"I find yours faultless and, as I only exchanged a few words with Henriet, I cannot speak about her."

"Then again that is a compliment I will treasure," Caterina said, "and I cannot tell you how happy I am that you are not as angry as I expected you to be. In fact I should congratulate you on making 'the best of a bad job'."

"The question I want to put," the Duke replied, "is must it be a bad one?"

Caterina did not pretend to misunderstand him.

"I don't know the answer to that and nor do you. We can only find out as we travel on this magnificent ship and please, please now that I have left my cabin can I see all over the ship?"

"Is that what you have been wanting to do?" the Duke asked.

"I have been longing for it. I love ships and this is quite the most awesome one I have ever seen."

"Very well. It must be nearly dinnertime now and I hope you will dine with me. Tomorrow morning I will take you round the whole Battleship and show you all the improvements that made have been made to the Ironclads."

He smiled at her before he continued,

"When we reach England, I will take you on a voyage on my new yacht which has just been finished. I intend to sail it to Cowes this year."

"I have heard about Cowes," Caterina said, "and how the Prince of Wales is the Head of the Yacht Club."

"It is something I feel quite sure you will enjoy."

"I know I will, but I never thought in my wildest dreams that you or anyone else would ever take me there."

"I go there every year and as my wife you will, of course, attend all the smart parties given in honour of the Prince of Wales. Actually I intend to win a few prizes."

"That will be exciting and something new. Tell me what else is waiting for you in London."

"I think that will take a long time," the Duke said.

At this point a Steward announced that dinner was served.

Caterina found she much enjoyed all the dishes the English chef provided for them to eat together with some delicious wine the Duke told her he had brought on board from his own cellars.

Conversation during dinner could not, of course, be at all intimate and, as soon as it was over, Caterina returned to her cabin.

To her surprise and great relief, she found herself doing so quite reluctantly.

*

The next morning, after breakfast in her own cabin, Caterina went on deck to meet the Duke.

"Come along," he said, "and I will introduce you to the Captain, who you rudely ignored when you arrived."

"I was taking great trouble that you would not see my face and it was not easy, especially when I was obliged to remove the veil."

"You deceived me and you deceived a great many other people. I only hope that you will not have any reason to deceive me again in the future."

"I hope not too. I was terrified that you would find out what was happening before the wedding could take place."

She gave a little sign of relief.

"Now, she said, "I am longing to see the ship as you promised."

"That is what you will do, so do come along."

They walked round the Battleship and Caterina's enthusiasm delighted the Captain and the crew.

The Duke saw at once that she had been well very trained at smiling and in being pleasant to the people who were introduced to her, and he was impressed when she shook hands with every one of the crew and had something personal to say to them all.

She thanked the chef for the meals she had actually not eaten, as Malca had brought her food from the Palace, but she was so charming to him that the Duke was aware that he would strive in every possible way to make the dishes more exciting than they had been previously.

Finally they went up on deck and Caterina walked to the bow of the ship to watch the waves breaking over it.

"I am not the least surprised," she said to the Duke, "that the Russians were frightened when six Battleships as large as this one appeared up the Dardanelles."

"And we must continue to frighten them and don't forget that you have been used as a safeguard against their infiltration."

"Only a very small one and I would really like to be as big, important and formidable as this Battleship is."

The Duke laughed.

"I think that is very unlikely, but you have certainly scared me. I will always wonder in the future what you are planning and fear I am not clever enough to catch you out."

Caterina looked at him quickly to see if he was serious or teasing her and, as she was not certain which it was, she responded,

"If I promise to try to do what you want me to, will you believe me?"

"I believe you are capable of anything," the Duke remarked. "If I am honest, I would rather you were with me than against me!"

"Then I do promise never to be against you again, because you have been so kind and far more understanding than I thought you would be."

"Were you really very scared of me?" he asked.

Caterina nodded.

"I lay awake terrified by the thought of what you might say and do when you learnt the truth."

"I have to admit that you are a brilliant actress, but please never try to act in front of me in future. I want to have the truth from you – and the whole truth."

"That is what I will try to give you," Caterina said. "I know Henriet will be as happy as I am that it has all gone off so well."

"I just cannot quite understand," the Duke enquired, "how she was brave enough to marry a man who would not be accepted by her father or I imagine the people he reigns over."

"I don't think they would really mind so much, but if Uncle Adolphus had known she wanted to marry a man who was only a soldier and of no social standing, I think he would not only have been extremely angry but would have literally dragged Henriet up the aisle to become your wife."

"And she wanted to die rather than do that?"

Caterina nodded.

"I was not exaggerating when I told you what she threatened to do. She had a revolver and would not have given it up if I had not promised I would take her place at the altar."

"The whole story seems to me incredible. At the same time I do consider myself very fortunate to have you, rather than a girl who is in love with someone else."

Suddenly he stopped.

"I did not ask you," he said, "if you are in love with anyone. Perhaps that is a question I should have asked you first."

"If I had been, I would have told you," Caterina replied. "I have always wanted to be in love, but it has just never happened."

She gave a sigh before she went on,

"You see in Theiss we are much more countrified than they are in Istria and, while I have been out riding and shooting with my father, I have not met many young men."

"So you have never been kissed?"

Caterina shook her head.

"One man tried it at a ball when we were sitting out in the conservatory, but he was middle-aged with a wife."

The Duke smiled.

"Then it's the sad, sad story of Cinderella who has not enjoyed life as she should have done."

"That is just not so," Caterina countered. "I have enjoyed every minute of being with Papa. He is extremely amusing and most intelligent. And while his friends have treated me as a little girl, they were always interesting to listen to and I learnt a great deal from them."

"So your brain is older than it might be at your age," the Duke declared.

"I hope so. I promise I will try, if you will help me, to learn all about England and what English Society will expect of your wife."

"They will expect you to help me and to have, shall we say, an affection for those we employ and who live on my estate, where the Dukes of Dunlerton have reigned, as one might boast, for many generations."

"So you have a little Kingdom of your own!"

"That is how I like to think of it and, as you will be its Queen, they will all look to you for guidance, sympathy and understanding."

Caterina laughed and then, as he looked at her in surprise, she said,

"Now you sound exactly like Mama. That is just the sort of thing she used to say and everyone in Theiss adored her because she was always ready to help them if she could. She spent more time than any other Princess in visiting the hospitals, the schools and the homes of poorer and less fortunate people."

"I see you have been brought up in exactly the right way," the Duke said. "And it is something I always hoped to find in my wife."

Caterina was silent for a moment and then she said,

"I find it difficult to think of myself as your wife. So please will you be very patient with me and tell me what I have to do so that I don't make any silly mistakes."

"I think if you just behave naturally you will not make any mistakes, but if you do, I promise to forgive you!"

He smiled at her and Caterina smiled back.

"That is what I want to hear," she murmured.

Then she gave a little cry.

"Oh, look, I am sure that is Brindisi ahead of us. I did not think that we would arrive until nightfall."

"We have been steaming very fast and, as I have to return to England quickly, we cannot stay here for long."

"We must leave Malca here and be certain that the message she expects from Henriet is waiting for her."

"So she is going to join her Mistress?"

"Yes! But because we are frightened that Uncle Adolphus will drag her back, it's best for you and me not to know where she is going. In fact, once she leaves this ship, we will have no contact with her."

"I see that you have arranged everything in your usual clever way and naturally I agree to everything you have said."

"She will be very happy that you are not angry with me as we feared you might be," Caterina told him. "And I don't mind, as I thought that I would, Malca going away, leaving me with no one to talk to."

"I hope you will talk to me," the Duke smiled.

"I want you to tell me everything I don't know about all the difficulties that England is encountering with her Dominions."

The Duke looked at her in surprise.

"Is that really of interest to you?" he asked.

"Of course it is. I have been reading all about the great Empire you now possess. As I have now become a British citizen by marriage, I want to know what you are doing and why. Also if you are really as perturbed by the Russians as we are."

The Duke mused again that she was really the most unusual young woman he had ever met.

He could not think of ever having a conversation with an older woman, let alone a girl of her age, who was really concerned about the workings of the British Empire.

Invariably they would talk only about themselves and expect him to say flattering words to them.

He had been pursued not only by young women but by their mothers ever since he could remember.

He had carefully avoided any female younger than thirty for the simple reason that he knew only too well that, if he paid them any attention at all, he would immediately encourage their parents to believe he was about to propose.

This was the reason why he had been so furious when Queen Victoria had sent for him and then told him abruptly he was to marry to please the Emperor of Austria!

He was engaged at the time in an *affaire-de-coeur* with an attractive married woman! And he was also being hotly pursued by the ambitious mother of the *debutante* of the Season, who was certainly very attractive.

Her father, who was very influential at Court, had decided that she should make the best and most illustrious marriage of the Season and it was inevitable that their eyes should turn towards him.

As he had told Caterina, he had no intention of marrying anyone for a very long time.

Yet it was quite impossible to refuse to obey Queen Victoria when she told him why he had been summoned to Windsor Castle.

"There is at the moment," Her Majesty had said, "no English Prince who is not married or not too young with whom I can answer the Emperor's request."

She paused while the Duke had drawn in his breath.

"But you, my dear Aden," she went on, "as we are all aware, are of Royal blood on your mother's side and the head of one of the most distinguished families in England."

"I have no wish, ma'am, to marry anyone," he had protested.

"Nonsense!" the Queen had replied. "You have to marry sooner or later and this is an opportunity that may not occur again. I have always been very fond of Prince Adolphus of Istria and his wife before she died. She was a charming and delightful woman."

She looked at the Duke sharply before she went on,

"I am quite sure that their daughter will make you an admirable wife and you will, at the very same time, be helping Austria and making the Russians aware that we disapprove of their behaviour in the Balkans."

Defying the Queen was impossible and the Duke had therefore been obliged to agree to her request.

It was only when he had left Windsor Castle that he had raged at being shackled for life, as he thought of it, and when he least expected it.

The beauty he had been having an *affaire-de-coeur* with had wept when he told her that he was leaving at once for Istria and then she had said,

"Don't let's be too depressed, dearest Aden. As soon as you return, I will be waiting for you. Your wife, being young and stupid, will have no idea why you have to spend so much time in London."

"I don't want to be married at all," the Duke had said angrily.

"I cannot think that any girl will interfere with us too much," the beauty had replied, "and, darling, we are wasting time now when you could be kissing me."

'I am trapped and bound,' the Duke had said to himself furiously as he had walked down the aisle with Caterina.

Yet now he found himself at dinner that evening laughing at Caterina's jokes and at the way she always had a quick answer to anything he said.

128

In fact, when he retired to bed in the somewhat uncomfortable cabin he had slept in for the last two nights, he was thinking that he had enjoyed this evening more than he had ever expected.

Before they bade each other 'goodnight', Caterina had said,

"Now that I don't have to hide from you any longer you must, of course, have the big cabin which belongs to the Captain and I will take the one you are using."

The Duke looked at her to see if she was speaking seriously.

He was thinking as he did so that any other woman would have made it obvious that the bed in the big cabin was meant for two people.

And then he realised that such a solution had never occurred to Caterina.

"Oh, I am quite all right where I am and it will not be long before we reach England," he replied to her. "All the rooms in my country house are large and exceedingly comfortable."

"I am sure they are," Caterina said. "It is just that I feel embarrassed at the idea of you squeezed into the small cabin while I have the much larger one."

"I promise you that the cabins in my yacht are very much more comfortable," the Duke replied, "but of course this is a ship of war."

"That is exactly what I said to Malca when they told me that they had no flowers for me."

The Duke made a mental note to give her flowers when they reached Brindisi.

They said 'goodnight' and the Duke went into his cabin.

He thought as he did so, that he was no longer as apprehensive about the future as he had been earlier and his marriage would not be as disagreeable as he thought it would be.

He was honest enough to admit that he had enjoyed the evening more than he had enjoyed a dinner *à deux* for a very long time.

'She is amazing,' he told himself. 'Quite amazing and so different from anything I ever expected.'

CHAPTER SEVEN

They arrived at Brindisi quite late that evening and Malca said that she would leave first thing in the morning.

"You must promise me," Caterina said, "that you will let me know when you arrive and thank you for all your wonderful help. And do persuade Henriet to tell me where she will be. She knows that I will not tell anyone and I don't want to lose touch with her."

"Of course not, Princess, and I'm sure she won't want to lose touch with you. After all you two have been together ever since you were babies."

Caterina then remembered that her Nanny had been good friends with Malca.

'I must not lose Henriet now,' she told herself, 'when I am going to a strange country where I will have no friends of my own.'

She tried not to let the thought depress her, equally she felt that she was skating on thin ice and at any moment might drop into dark cold misery.

But she was exceedingly relieved that the Duke was so different from what she had expected and that he had actually laughed at the situation they were in seemed to her a good omen.

She had thought he would take it very seriously, as undoubtedly her father and Prince Adolphus would do.

'I so wish there was an easy way out of this,' she thought to herself.

She knew what the simple answer was.

If Henriet had killed herself, as she had intended to do, there could have been no secret wedding and she would at this moment be on her way home to Theiss.

At the same time Caterina had to admit that she had enjoyed talking to the Duke over dinner.

That he had not raged or thrown her into the sea was certainly a step in the right direction.

The Battleship had by now moved slowly into the Port at Brindisi where there were only a few other ships.

"We will not stay long," the Duke said when she went into breakfast. "If you want to do any shopping or sightseeing, I suggest you do it quickly."

"I know, of course, that this is Italy, but also that here we are very close to Greece. I do so long one day to explore the whole of Greece and see Delos where Apollo was born."

"Do you really believe all those legends?" the Duke enquired.

"Of course I do. We were brought up on them and I always hoped that I would come with someone I love to Greece and especially to the Greek Islands."

She spoke in a dreamlike way that made the Duke look at her inquisitively.

Somehow he had not thought of her longing for love and now he realised that as a woman she was losing the excitement of falling in love and being wooed.

As every woman should be before she married.

It was something new for him to feel that he was a disappointment and yet he knew that was really the truth.

Caterina had sacrificed herself to save her friend from him and Austria from the Russians.

As he saw her smiling at the sunshine which was coming through the portholes, he thought that few women would have had the bravery to do what she had done and no woman of his acquaintance would ever be so optimistic about the future.

'I wonder if she still hates me,' he asked himself.

Looking back he realised how disagreeable he must have appeared to those two young girls.

"I tell you what we will do," he said aloud.

Caterina turned to look at him and he thought that her eyes were shining.

"I will take you ashore, because I want to buy you some flowers. I agree with you that the Battleship looks too austere if we are to pretend when we arrive in England that we are a devoted husband and wife."

"I hope our audience is not going to be too big too quickly," Catering replied. "It's a part I have never played before."

"Neither have I," the Duke concurred.

"Yes, but men are different. Of course you have had many beautiful ladies hanging on your word and then telling you how marvellous you are."

"Why should you say that?" he asked.

"Because it's very obvious that it has happened and naturally, like every other man in a top position, you have always asked yourself whether they wanted you because you are a Duke or because you are – handsome."

She hesitated a little over the last word and then she laughed and added,

"Of course I should be polite and say that the latter was the real reason."

"I think we promised that we would tell each other the truth," the Duke replied, "but, having been so cleverly deceived by you, I will always be suspicious, even if you tell me it's a fine day."

Caterina laughed.

"Well, it is and it's a very exciting day for me if I am to see what I know was a key town in Roman days."

"Well, hurry up and put on your hat or whatever you think is suitable for the occasion. The Captain will be furious if we are away for long."

"I am not afraid of the Captain," Caterina said as she reached the door. "Only that you might well steam off without me and then I will have to walk or swim home!"

As she ran along the passage, she heard the Duke laughing and she thought that if she was clever she must keep him laughing for as long as possible.

Otherwise there might be 'many a true word spoken in jest'.

The easiest way to be rid of her would be to put her down in some obscure place and it would take her weeks if not months to find her way home.

She had brought a little money with her, but it was only what she had expected to spend while she was in Istria with Henriet.

Her father had promised he would come and fetch her when she was ready to return home and so she had taken just enough money to tip the servants or to buy small necessities. For anything more expensive like a dress or a coat, she would ask for a bill to be sent home to be paid.

She looked very attractive in a summer hat, which matched her dress, when she joined the Duke on deck.

He had ordered an open carriage which was waiting for them on the Quay.

"We will have to hurry," he said, "for the simple reason that the Captain has just told me that he expects to go to the Far East as soon as he arrives back in London."

He paused a moment before he went on,

"In fact it is where he should have gone if he had not been ordered at a moment's notice to take me to Istria."

"And, of course, Her Majesty Queen Victoria has to be obeyed," Caterina said.

"Naturally," the Duke agreed.

"Are you intimidated by her?"

"Of course I am," the Duke replied. "Everyone is. But she has always been especially kind to me. She is my Godmother and so she looks on me as a child with a Royal relationship, who will always do as he is told."

Caterina laughed.

"It sounds very frightening."

"It can be and I am not looking forward to telling her about the dreadful mess I made of it in Istria."

Now he was speaking quite seriously and Caterina said in a soft voice,

"I am sorry, really very sorry for you. Something I never expected I would feel."

"I can see that I was a wicked ogre and the villain of the peace," the Duke sighed.

"Well, to be honest, you did rather behave like one. As I have told you, I was very scared of what you would say or do when I revealed myself as an imposter."

"And what do you feel now?" the Duke asked.

Caterina hesitated a moment.

"Go on, tell me the truth," he demanded, but with a distinct twinkle in his eyes.

"I was thinking," Caterina said, "that if I do, you might think I was sucking up to you, while, if I told you that you are still a menace, it would only be half true and one should not lie when one is thinking about Greece."

"So Greece is saving me. I have always thought it was different from other places."

"You have never been there?" she asked.

"I have wanted to, but, of course, I have read about the Gods and Goddesses and, although I was only young when I did, I have believed in them ever since."

Caterina clasped her hands together.

"You really do believe in them and it is the whole truth and nothing but the truth?"

"Of course it's the truth. There would be no use in my lying about it. I am totally certain that the Gods and Goddesses of Greece were very powerful and naturally I have always wanted to meet one."

"Just as I have wanted to meet Apollo. I suppose you cannot take me across to Greece now and we could explore the wonderful Temples. I am sure we should be thrilled to see with our very own eyes what we have always believed."

"I tell you what we will do," the Duke said. "I must allow the Captain to get back quickly to England, but later, when we have straightened out the mess we are in, I will take you to Greece. You will not only go to Delos but also to Delphi."

Caterina gave a cry of excitement.

"You promise me, you really promise me?"

"I promise on my honour."

"Then, if we hurry to England now, the sooner we can go to Greece!"

"I thought you would express it better than anyone else could," the Duke said.

The carriage stopped at a flower shop and the Duke climbed out.

He bought a huge amount of flowers, especially lilies, which were Caterina's favourite.

They were all piled into the carriage and then they drove back to the Port. Caterina was looking to the right and left and spoke very little.

The Duke, watching her, thought that it was strange to be with a beautiful woman, who, for the moment, had completely forgotten him – she was thinking only of the Classical Gods.

The Duke and Caterina arrived back at the ship and Caterina realised that, almost before they could pull up the gangway, they were moving out of the Port.

She went on deck to have her last glimpse of land and, if the Duke kept his promise, which she was sure he would, at least one of her dreams would come true.

Suddenly she remembered the lovely flowers they had bought and went below to help the Steward arrange them.

She kept the white lilies for her own cabin and put them in bowls on each side of the bed.

Later, when she told the Duke where they were, she said,

"Now I feel very like a bride and I am so grateful to you for giving me such glorious flowers."

"I suppose," the Duke asked, "you remembered to bring the pearl and diamond necklace away with you."

"Actually I did. I hesitated as to whether I should wear it the first night we had dinner together, but I thought the mere fact that I was wearing it instead of Henriet would annoy you."

"It has been in my family for two hundred years. My mother always wore it and I would like you to wear it tonight."

"Thank you," Caterina sighed, "I shall be proud to. It's the most beautiful necklace I have ever seen."

"There are a lot more jewels in the safe in London which I hope you will enjoy, also some in the country."

"I am longing to see your country house," Caterina said. "Do you have really good horses?"

The Duke smiled.

"Yes, they are exceptional and I suppose you will now tell me that you are an outstanding rider."

"I should be, because Papa owns some of the best horses in the whole of Austria."

"I had no idea."

"He has won a great number of races with them," Caterina said. "He himself is said to be one of the finest horsemen in the whole country and he loves his horses so much that, when I was a little girl, I always used to wonder who came first, Mama or his favourite stallion."

"Then I think your father will admire mine when he sees them," the Duke said. "I will feel extremely frustrated if he says they are not as good as his!"

"Now you can understand that I have been riding almost before I left the cradle."

"That is one thing we certainly have in common."

Caterina did not answer and after a moment he said,

"But I did not expect that you would enjoy reading as well."

"I cannot think why not. I am enjoying enormously the book your valet gave me, which is all about India and other countries in the East."

The Duke looked at her.

"Are you expecting me to take you to India as well as to Greece?"

"It would be a wonderful experience for me. I have read and read about the countries of the East, but have never had a chance to leave Austria."

"Then that is certainly something we should do in the future. I love travelling, but I have yet to meet a woman who wants to travel far and who does not complain when she does."

"I will certainly not complain and I am prepared to ride anything you provide me with, even if it is an elephant or a dromedary!"

The Duke laughed.

"You may have to do both or perhaps end up with nothing more exciting than a rather reluctant mule."

"If it has four legs, I will be thrilled with it!"

Then unexpectedly she sighed.

"What is worrying you?" the Duke asked.

"I am just thinking that, if the Queen is really angry at what has happened, she might make me stay in Windsor Castle as a Lady-in-Waiting or something like that, so that I will be taught the proper way to behave with someone as distinguished as you."

The Duke thought it was a rather intelligent matter that she was raising.

"I think that is very unlikely and, as I have been a courtier for many years, the Queen will expect me to teach you all you have to know about behaviour at Court."

He was aware that Caterina's eyes lit up.

"That will be splendid," she said. "I promise you that I learn quickly and we need not waste too much time curtseying, kowtowing and addressing people in the right way when we might be out riding."

"There I agree with you, but I warn you I will be a very strict and impatient teacher."

Caterina grinned.

"And I will be a very obedient pupil, but at times I may play truant!"

He thought this was a slightly absurd conversation, but one he found himself unexpectedly enjoying.

Caterina was rather disappointed when she learnt that Marseilles would not be on their direct route home.

"I want to stand on French soil just to say I have," she complained.

"I am sorry, but the Captain says he will stop only at Gibraltar and you must make do with that."

"Oh, I would love to go to Gibraltar! Papa told me they make the most beautiful embroidered shawls based on old Chinese patterns."

"They do," the Duke replied, "and I have seen the originals in China. I hope you will see them one day."

"Oh, that would be very thrilling. I would love to go to China."

"I think you would find it rather rough," the Duke replied, "and that you would enjoy Japan more."

Caterina drew in her breath.

"Are these just make-believe dreams or will they come true?" she asked.

"I can promise you they will come true, although you may have to wait a little. Undoubtedly we will go to these places one day and I will be interested to see if they come up to your expectations."

"Then I will be counting the days, the hours and the minutes until we can go!" Caterina almost exploded.

"And what about the horses?" the Duke asked her. "We cannot take them with us."

"No, but they must wait their turn. I am actually beginning to wonder if you are real or merely part of my dreams."

The Duke did not answer this.

Then they were chattering away about the histories of China and Japan, about which, to his surprise, Caterina knew a great deal.

*

Finally they reached London, steaming both by day and by night and the Duke thought they had been quicker than he had ever imagined possible.

"What are we going to do when we arrive at the Port of London?" Caterina asked him.

"It's not a question of 'we'," the Duke replied. "I will go at once to see the Queen and then I will have another suggestion to make, which I hope you will find interesting."

"Please tell me now," Caterina begged.

"No, because it may not come true and then you would be disappointed."

"Now you are making me unbearably curious. It's not fair that I will have to sit and wait patiently and count the hours and the minutes until you return from Windsor Castle."

"I promise that I will be as quick as I can. What I do have to tell you now and what may sound surprising is that you are not to wait here on the Battleship."

"May I not go to your town house?"

The Duke shook his head.

"No, because no one must know we are in London until I have told the Queen what has happened. But I have given orders for my yacht to be ready where we disembark and I want you to wait in it until I return from The Castle."

"I don't mind doing that, as I am sure your yacht is very smart and up to date. I always wanted Papa to buy a new one, but he was quite happy with his old one."

"Well, my yacht is new and I hope that you will be impressed by it," the Duke said.

*

Having arrived late at night, they slept on board the Battleship and then left immediately after breakfast.

It was, in fact, only eight o'clock when the Duke took Caterina aboard *The Shooting Star*.

It was moored just a short distance from where the Battleship had anchored and one glance at it told Caterina that it was even smarter than she had expected.

The Duke introduced the Captain to her without saying who she was and then he departed immediately for Windsor Castle.

He was driving a team he had bought recently and which his Head Groom had taken to the yacht for him.

Looking at them from the yacht, Caterina longed to be beside the Duke when he drove off and she was certain that he would go faster than she had ever driven before.

His horses were perfectly matched and were, she recognised, outstanding.

Then she told herself that she was seeing a life she had never seen before and must not complain.

At the same time she realised that the Duke was feeling anxious about his visit to the Queen.

She could not help sensing that he was afraid, as he had told her when she first revealed who she was, that he would be a laughing-stock for having married the wrong woman.

Being perceptive, she could understand his friends and acquaintances laughing at him in all the smart Clubs in

London and the Dowagers and social beauties would all snigger about it in their grand houses.

'It's not his fault,' she reflected. 'The Queen sent him out to Istria to marry Henriet without even asking him if he was willing to have an Austrian wife.'

But now she realised that he was in a predicament that could hurt him considerably.

As she stood on deck and watched the barges and ships moving slowly up and down the Thames, she prayed that it would not be as bad as he anticipated.

She knew only too well how important the Queen was, not only in England but all over the world.

Of course her command must be obeyed, however much an individual might suffer in doing so.

'Oh, please God let her tell him that he did the right thing and don't let him be laughed at by all his friends let alone his enemies,' she prayed.

The sun was shining on the river and Caterina felt as if the light that seemed for the moment to blind her eyes was an answer from Heaven.

It would not be as bad as she feared.

Yet the hours seemed to go by very slowly and she found it difficult to do anything but watch the traffic on the river.

Even the books that filled a huge bookcase in one of the cabins could not distract her from worrying over the Duke.

It suddenly struck her how very strange it was that, having both hated him and feared him, she had these last days enjoyed being with him more than she could possibly put into words.

The sea had been rough after they left Gibraltar, but not, however, so rough that she had to stay in her cabin.

She had been thrilled with the shawl the Duke had bought her and she wore it every evening to show him how lovely it was. It was a present she had greatly appreciated, being unlike any shawl she had ever seen.

They had talked and laughed in a way that she had never expected from the Duke.

Now she was feeling half afraid that in some way the Queen might break up their marriage or get it annulled and even as she thought of it she was surprised at herself.

Then she knew, although it seemed incredible, that she had no wish to leave the Duke.

She wanted to be with him, to talk to him and have him showing her all he had promised to show her.

'This is a real adventure,' she now told herself, 'an adventure that I had never expected to have. It's very very different from anything I have known before.'

She thought that the Duke might be back early in the afternoon, but, when he did not come, she suddenly felt afraid.

Perhaps after all, the Queen was shocked and angry at the way she had taken Henriet's place.

She might insist on her returning home and annul the marriage that should never have taken place.

It was then that Caterina admitted to herself that she not only wanted to stay but she wanted to be with the Duke and she wanted to know him far, far better than she did at the moment.

She looked down at the wedding ring on her finger and told herself that it was a fake. It had been put there under false pretences and she ought really to throw it into the river.

'Why is he so long? What can have happened?' she asked herself.

Then she was praying again that it would not be as bad as she and the Duke feared.

It was nearly five o'clock when, looking through the trees along the Embankment, she saw in the distance the horses the Duke was driving.

For a moment she was afraid that she might be imagining them. Then as they came nearer she knew that it was the Duke.

At last he was coming back!

Her first impulse was to run to the gangway to meet him and then, because she was afraid of what he might have to tell her, she went into the Saloon.

It seemed to her as if a century passed before the horses drew up and the Duke came aboard.

Then she heard his voice speaking to someone.

A moment later the door of the Saloon opened.

It was then, as she saw him come in through the door, which he closed behind him, that the strict control she had been keeping over herself broke.

She ran to him and threw herself against him.

"What has happened? What has gone wrong? Why have you been – so long?" she asked.

The words were falling from her as if she had no control over them.

For a moment he looked down at her.

Then, drawing her close to him, his lips were on hers.

Caterina could not believe it was happening.

Then a strange feeling she had never known before began to course through her, as the Duke drew her closer still and his lips became more demanding.

He kissed her until it was impossible for her to speak or even think.

Then he said,

"It's all right, my darling, everything is all right. Now we are going away on our honeymoon."

Because he had kissed her so intensely, she could hardly understand what he was saying.

As she looked up, their eyes met and there was a radiance in hers that he had not seen before.

He kissed her again.

Then, as they felt the engines beneath them begin to turn, the Duke drew her to the sofa.

He sat down with his arm still around her.

"Is it really all right?" Caterina asked in a whisper.

"Everything is fine. Now, my darling, I can tell you what I have wanted to say for the last ten days, which have seemed like a thousand years, that I love you."

He kissed her once again so that it was impossible for Caterina to answer.

She knew, as an ecstasy swept through her body and into her lips, that she loved him as he had said he loved her.

*

It seemed a long time later, but it was actually only a short while before the yacht was heading downstream.

"Now – you must tell me – what has happened?" Caterina asked.

"All I can think about at the moment is kissing you as I have wanted to do for so long," the Duke said. "How can you be so beautiful and so ecstatically lovely?"

"I have been so worried – and I did not realise – it was because I loved you – until you kissed me."

The Duke smiled.

"I have so much to teach you, my darling, and it's going to take a very long time."

"Why are we moving?" Caterina asked him.

"I will tell you the whole story, but all I can think about at present is you and how utterly and completely perfect you are."

"Are you really saying this to me?" Caterina asked.

"I have much more to say to you, but I suppose you must know first what has happened at Windsor Castle."

"Was the Queen shocked and disagreeable?"

"She was marvellous," the Duke replied, "and I respect and admire her more than I have ever done before. And that is saying a great deal."

"But why? What has she done?"

"I went ahead and told her the whole truth about what had happened.   It was the only thing I could do,"

"You mean that you told her about Henriet running away because she was in love?"

"I told her that and that she was married before I actually married you. I explained that I had no idea I was not marrying the Princess she had sent me out to marry."

"Was she angry?"

"No. I told her you had taken your friend's place in order to save her life," the Duke replied.

"Was she angry about that?"

"She thought it was very brave and heroic of you and I believe when you do meet her she will congratulate you."

Caterina stared at him in amazement.

Then he went on,

"It took a little time, but Her Majesty has thought of an explanation for me to use, which I have to admit is extremely clever."

"Tell me! Please tell me!" Caterina pleaded.

"That is what I am trying to do, but I keep thinking how beautiful you are and how much I want to kiss you. Then I forget what I was going to say."

"You must tell me. I have been so frightened that Her Majesty would be angry with you."

"She was not angry, but determined that she and she alone should solve the problem and she has done so."

"But how?"

"Her Majesty's story is that, when I arrived at Istria I was told secretly by you and Henriet that she was already married to the man she loved. But you were prepared to take her place for the sake of Austria and, of course, of Istria, which is so coveted by the Russians because of its access to the sea."

Caterina was listening wide-eyed.

"No one else knew what was happening and Prince Adolphus was completely and utterly in the dark."

The yacht was by now in the centre of the river and, as it gained speed, Caterina moved nearer to the Duke.

He put his arms round her and then pulled her close against him as he continued,

"Her Majesty has already invited Prince Adolphus and your father to come to Windsor Castle."

Caterina gave a little gasp.

"My father!" she exclaimed.

"Her Majesty is going to tell them that this is what has happened and that they must agree to her suggestion of what she considers to be the only way of dealing with the situation and make the Russians realise that Istria is under the protection of Britain."

"What does she suggest?" Caterina asked.

"It will be announced almost immediately that the Duchess of Dunlerton has contracted a seriously unpleasant Eastern fever, which regrettably proved fatal."

Caterina gave a little gasp, but did not interrupt.

"She has been buried at sea and, as we were on our honeymoon when it happened, I will disappear, being in mourning, into the East where I have been before.

"It is there, quite by chance, that I meet the Princess Caterina of Theiss and fall in love with her. The people of Istria, who had deeply mourned their Princess, will be very delighted when we visit Istria later in the year."

"Do you think that Papa and Prince Adolphus will agree to that idea?" Caterina asked a little breathlessly.

"I think actually, they have no alternative," the Duke said. "And if you write and tell your father that you are going to stay with friends in Japan, he will, I am certain, want you to enjoy your visit to the East."

"And when we return?" Caterina asked.

"You will be welcomed with open arms in Theiss and, because you were such a very close friend of Princess Henriet, you will also be very welcome in Istria."

The Duke's voice deepened before he added,

"What is more the Russians will know that both Istria and Theiss have the blessing of Queen Victoria."

"It's clever, very clever," Caterina said. "In fact, it is the cleverest scheme I have ever heard and Henriet can disappear and live happily ever after with Fritz and not have a worry in the world. At the same time you are still landed with *me*!"

The Duke laughed and pulled her closer.

"I have exactly what I always wanted. We have all the time we want to spend on our honeymoon and I can show you the East as you have always wanted to go there."

"Is this true or am I dreaming?" Caterina asked.

"It's really true, my darling. But we have to keep out of sight until we can announce our marriage. Then you will see how grand and important you are as the Duchess of Dunlerton."

"Oh, you are wonderful!" Caterina exclaimed. "I was so afraid that the Queen would insist on our marriage being annulled."

"I would not have let her do that. I think I began to fall in love with you the moment I first saw you and was extremely angry that I was being made to marry Henriet instead of you."

He gave her a loving smile before he went on,

"But now I have come to know and love you, I will kill any man who tries to separate us from each other."

"Do you really feel like that?" Caterina asked him.

"I do and a great deal more. I intend, my precious, to teach you all about love, which you will find far more fascinating than learning about the protocol of the Royal Household."

His eyes were smiling as he spoke and Caterina put her head on his shoulder.

"I did not realise until you kissed me," she said, "that I was in love with you, but now I know it is the most marvellous thing that has ever happened to me that we are married."

"We are married, my darling, and nothing and no one will ever part us. You made the supreme sacrifice for your friend and you have found my love instead! God does work in mysterious ways sometimes!"

Then he was kissing her once again, kissing her so wildly and demandingly that she felt as if he was carrying her up into the sky.

*

Later that night the yacht was anchored in a quiet bay so that there was no movement.

The Duke came into the Master cabin of the yacht, where Caterina was already waiting for him in the bed.

It was far more attractive than her cabin had been on the Battleship. The curtains over the portholes were of a rose-coloured chintz and there were flowers in the cabin, although only a few.

The Duke had promised that they would stop at the first Port of call and Caterina should have all the lilies he could buy.

Caterina was not at this moment thinking of lilies but of her husband.

As he came into the cabin, she thought that no one could look more handsome and masculine.

'I love him! I adore him!' she said to herself over and over again. 'Everything is just how I dreamt it would be – and even better.'

The Duke came to her side of the bed and stood for the moment looking down at her.

"Are you real?" he asked. "I began to dream of this soon after we left Istria and now it has come true, just as it does in the Fairy stories."

"This is a Fairy story," Caterina said. "When you kissed me today, I knew that it was something I had been praying for and wanting for a long time."

"You will never have to pray for it again."

He then turned out the lights and pulled back the curtains so that the moonlight poured in to turn the cabin to silver.

Then, as he climbed into the bed and held Caterina close to him, he said,

"Now we can feel that we are floating on a star and are going to enjoy, as we travel the world, the perfect love we have both dreamt of. Through God's mercy we have finally both found it and it is *ours*."

"I love you, I adore you, Aden," she whispered.

Then he was kissing her.

Kissing her at first so gently and then demandingly and possessively.

He kissed her until Caterina was certain that they were touching the stars.

When he made her his, they passed into the Heaven which God had made for lovers and which would be theirs for all Eternity and they would never ever part.